The Seeds of Murder

by the same author

The Silent Liars
Shem's Demise
A Trout in the Milk
Reward for a Defector
A Pinch of Snuff
The Juror
Menaces, Menaces
Murder with Malice
The Fatal Trip
Crooked Wood
Anything but the Truth
Smooth Justice
Victim of Circumstance
A Clear Case of Suicide
Crime Upon Crime
Double Jeopardy
Hand of Fate
Goddess of Death
A Party to Murder
Death in Camera
The Hidden Man
Death at Deepwood Grange
The Uninvited Corpse
The Injudicious Judge
Dual Enigma
A Compelling Case
Rosa's Dilemma
A Dangerous Business

THE
SEEDS
OF
MURDER

Michael Underwood

St. Martin's Press
New York

Library of Congress Cataloging-in-Publication Data

Underwood, Michael.
    The seeds of murder / Michael Underwood.
        p.   cm.
    ISBN 0-312-07800-5
    I. Title.
  PR6055.V3S44   1992
  823'.914—dc20   92-131
                                                                          CIP

First published in Great Britain by Macmillan London Limited.

First U.S. Edition: May 1992
10 9 8 7 6 5 4 3 2 1

PART I

1

It was summer 1932. A succession of sultry days and stiflingly hot nights had left the staff of Warren Hall School with frayed nerves and shortened tempers. For their part the boys (ages eight to thirteen) displayed longer than usual bouts of torpor and briefer than usual periods of manic activity.

Mr Iredale (nicknamed the Airedale) who taught French to Form 1A had never found it easy to keep order and had long been aware that he was not cut out to teach ten and eleven year olds the mysteries of *accents graves* and *accents aigus* or to explain why the word for sea should be feminine and that for ocean masculine, except that it was so.

'Did you know, sir, that in German the sun is feminine and the moon masculine?' a particularly irritating boy asked on a particularly hot afternoon. 'Did you, sir?'

'We're here to learn French not German,' the master replied acerbically and turned back to the blackboard. A second later he wheeled round and glared at fourteen innocent faces staring at him. 'Who did that?' he asked angrily.

'Did what, sir?' enquired a boy named Bostock.

'You know perfectly well. Who flicked that . . . that missile just now?'

The missile in question had been an ink-sodden pellet of blotting-paper discharged by an elastic band. Its target had been the back of Mr Iredale's head, but it had sailed past his ear and plopped damply against the blackboard.

There was no answer and the Airedale went on, 'Was it you Willett?'

The boy so addressed was sitting in the middle of the second row of desks.

'Me, sir? I've not done anything.' His tone was almost disdainful.

'Who saw Willett do it?' the master asked and when no reply was forthcoming went on, 'Very well, the whole form will be kept in on Saturday afternoon.'

'But, sir . . .' an outraged chorus burst out.

'There are no buts. Either the boy in question owns up or you all suffer.' As he spoke he glanced hard at Stephen Willett, who sat staring impassively ahead of him. Though he knew perfectly well who had flicked the blotting-paper pellet, schoolboy honour forbade sneaking, which was the most heinous offence in their code.

The afternoon lesson came to an end and the form was dismissed, some to go and play cricket and others to swim.

'I'll see you all here on Saturday afternoon,' Mr Iredale said grimly as they put away their books. 'That is, unless the guilty boy owns up before prayers this evening.' He gave Willett a final accusing stare before sweeping out of the room.

As soon as he had gone a number of boys turned on Gunning, an overweight boy who was sitting at his desk with a pleased smirk on his face.

'Go on, Gunning, you've got to own up. It's not fair we should all be kept in.'

Gunning shrugged. 'The Airedale thinks it was Willett, so let him own up.'

'Why should I own up to something I didn't do?' Willett asked with a touch of indignation.

Gunning gave another shrug. 'It's up to you. I don't mind spending Saturday afternoon here. It'll be cooler than standing about on a cricket field. Anyway, I hate cricket.'

'We could tell the Airedale it was you,' someone piped up.

'I'd deny it. And later I'd bash your head in.' Gunning was not averse to using bullying tactics to solve problems with boys smaller than himself.

It was at this point that Stephen Willett decided he might as well accept the blame for the misdirected pellet. It would save everyone trouble in the long run. He would almost certainly be caned by the headmaster, but that wouldn't be the first time. He was fed up with school, anyway, and didn't much mind what happened.

2

'Hello, young Willett. Hear you got your backside tanned yesterday. Hurt much?'

'No more than usual.'

Joe Atherly chuckled. He was only eighteen himself and was the school's odd-job boy, giving a hand wherever it was required.

He had caught up with Stephen Willett who was wandering about alone on the farther side of the cricket field.

'Funny kid, aren't you?' Joe went on cheerfully.

'No.'

'Don't seem to have any friends, do you?' Willett shrugged and Joe continued, 'When I was your age, I had dozens of friends. Now I've got a girl-friend. Like girls, do you?'

'Not especially.'

Joe grinned. 'You will one day. Anyway, what are you doing over here on your own?'

'Nothing special.'

'I'm on my way to help Wally Price cut up a dead tree in the copse.'

'Who's Wally Price?'

'Lives in a caravan on other side of village. You'll know his face when you see him. He does quite a lot of jobs round here. You can come and give us a hand if you want.'

'I don't mind watching you.'

Just then a man broke cover from the copse and came toward them.

'Here's Wally now,' Joe said. As Price reached them, Joe made the introduction. 'This is young Willett. He got a tanning yesterday from the headmaster.'

'Let's see the marks,' Price said with interest.

'No.'

'I'll give you sixpence.'

'No.'

'Go on. No need to be shy.'

'No.' This time Willett spoke with a touch of rising anger.

9

'All right, if you don't want to . . . Come on, Joe, let's get on with that tree.'

'Do you really live in a caravan?' Willett asked suddenly.

'Yes. Joe told you, did he?'

'Where is it?'

'Why d'you want to know?' Price asked suspiciously.

'I just wondered.'

'T'other side of Greenborough Common, if you must know.'

'Do you live there all the year round?'

'Near enough. My mum and dad live in the village and I sometimes go back there for a night or two. Why are you so interested in where I live?'

'I know somebody else who lives in a caravan.'

'Here in Greenborough?'

'No. At home.'

'Lots of folk live in caravans.'

They had reached the edge of the copse and Stephen Willett paused. 'I don't think I'll come any further,' he said and turned on his heels.

'He's a rum kid, that one,' Joe remarked. 'Always gets picked on by the others.'

'What did you say his name was?' Price asked.

'Willett.'

3

'Blenkin?'

'Here.'

'Catherwood?'

'Here.'

'Gunning?'

'Here.'

Morning roll-call, taken by forms, was followed by prayers, then breakfast.

Form 1A answered to their names and trooped into chapel. The master taking the roll-call reached the last name.

'Willett?'

There was no answer and he glanced up with an exasperated frown.

'Willett?' he called out in a slightly louder voice. But there was still no response. He turned to a younger master who was hovering nearby.

'Go and see if you can find him. He may still be asleep in his cubicle. Some boys'll sleep through the second coming.'

The younger man smiled and hurried away. He returned after a few minutes to report that Stephen Willett wasn't in his cubicle, though his bed had been slept in.

'What about the lavatories? He may be hiding there.'

The master shook his head. 'No. I've looked.'

'Well, there's nothing more we can do at the moment. I'll let the headmaster know as soon as prayers are over.'

Mr Thurston had been headmaster of Warren Hall School for ten years, his father having founded it at the turn of the century. In the fullness of time he would hand it on to his own son who was currently in his final year at Cambridge.

He listened gravely when told of Willett's absence. He hated boys running away, it gave the school a bad name whatever their motive. When Willett came back, he could expect to be punished, but, meanwhile, where was he?

As soon as the boys were seated in the dining-hall and before the daily platefuls of grey but nourishing porridge were ladled out, he called for silence.

'Has anybody seen Willett this morning?' he asked, surveying the rows of small faces turned in his direction, some lively and eager, others indelibly stupid. A number of hands shot up.

'Yes, Noakes?'

'I saw him last night, sir.'

'I did say *this morning*, Noakes. Anyway, what time last night?'

'When we went up to bed, sir.'

'Perhaps Onslow could throw light on the matter, sir,' said a bespectacled boy who was well on the way to becoming a full-blown pedant. 'He sleeps in the next cubicle to Willett.'

Onslow turned slowly pink as attention focused on him. He shook his head.

'No-o, sir,' he stammered.

'No, sir, what?' Mr Thurston enquired testily.

'Just no, sir.'

'Did you hear Willett moving about in the night?'

'Definitely not, sir.'

'And you never saw him this morning?'

'No, sir.'

'What about you, Cuckfield; you sleep on his other side?'

The boy so addressed shook his head almost curtly.

'I didn't see or hear anything, sir,' he said with a touch of disdain.

It was soon apparent that an explanation for Willett's absence would not be forthcoming from any of the boys. This didn't mean, however, that their capacity for rumour-mongering would be in any way diminished.

'I'd better phone his grandfather,' Mr Thurston said to his wife with a heavy sigh when breakfast was over. 'He's his guardian. It's possible he may know something.'

'From all I gather, Stephen goes his own way in the school holidays. His grandfather's too old to take a proper interest in him. It can be hard on boys whose parents live abroad. And India is such a terribly long way off.'

'The last letter I had from Willett's father mentioned that his own father wasn't in the best of health.'

'What'll you do, if the grandfather can't help?'

Mr Thurston sucked thoughtfully at his lower lip. 'I suppose I'll have to notify the police,' he said with a further sigh. 'I'll call the chief constable myself. That'll ensure the matter is handled discreetly. The last thing we want is any kind of scandal. We must still hope that Willett will suddenly turn up.' In a pensive tone he added, 'I confess I don't understand that boy, and it's not often you've heard me make that admission.'

'No, dear,' his wife said dutifully. The truth was that she was more adept than her husband at understanding boys who didn't fit the conventional mould. Personally she had a soft spot for Stephen Willett. He was a dreamy, self-contained child and she saw him becoming an explorer when he grew up. He had seemed rather pleased when she once told him this.

4

Three days later the mystery of Stephen Willett's disappearance was nowhere nearer a solution.

The police were now on the scene and school buildings and grounds had been searched inch by inch for clues. Staff and boys had all been questioned, but nobody seemed able to shed any light on where he could be and why he had gone. School life had inevitably been disrupted and the headmaster and his wife spent a great deal of time fending off enquiries from parents and press.

Each day produced a fresh batch of rumours from boys with imaginations as vivid as that of Jules Verne. The latest was that Willett had been abducted by members of an Indian sect who came from the state in which his father was a senior political adviser. It had not travelled far before being embellished to the effect that the hapless Willett was being held in a cellar guarded by venomous snakes. As the rumour grew, so did the size of the snakes.

Detective Inspector Stadden, who had been assigned to the enquiry by the chief constable, found himself drowning in a sea of speculation without a single concrete lead to develop.

'Is the boy alive or dead?' the chief constable asked bluntly when Stadden was making his report on the third day of the enquiry.

'I'd say alive, sir.'

'Is that because you've found no evidence to the contrary?'

'Yes, sir.'

'It's hardly conclusive.'

'I agree, sir. But I'm at least satisfied that the boy left the school of his own accord. There's no evidence anywhere of a struggle having taken place and it's inconceivable that he could have been forcibly abducted without waking up some of the boys in his dormitory.'

'That seems logical. Would he have had any problem getting out of the building?'

'No. In view of the hot weather, a good many windows have been left open all night.'

13

'I suppose someone could have been waiting outside for him?'

'That's one possibility, sir. The other is that he went to visit a local person.'

The chief constable frowned. 'Explain.'

'I've not yet had an opportunity of following this up, as the information only reached me just before I left to come here.' He paused. 'There's a youth called Joe Atherly who does odd jobs at the school. There's also a man named Walter Price who lives in a caravan on the outskirts of Greenborough. It seems that two days before he disappeared, Willett was introduced to Price by Atherly. Price and Atherly had instructions to cut up a fallen tree. On his way to the scene Atherly came across Willett who was wandering about in the area. He knew Willett had been caned the previous day and asked him about it . . .'

'Asked him about it?' the chief constable broke in in a disapproving tone.

'Asked him whether it had hurt,' Stadden explained.

'Don't like the sound of that! Not the sort of question Atherly should have been asking. Shows an unhealthy interest in something he shouldn't be interested in at all.'

Stadden drew a deep breath as he prepared to reveal details that the chief constable could only regard as even more sinister.

'I agree, sir,' he said solemnly. 'Most undesirable, and I'm afraid that wasn't all. It appears that Price offered the boy sixpence to show him the marks on his backside.'

'And?' the chief constable enquired in an ominous tone.

'Willett refused.'

'What do you know about this fellow Price? He sounds to me like a pervert.'

'I've spoken to the village constable at Greenborough and he says that he knows Price, though he hasn't been in any trouble with the police. He has a reputation for chasing girls and entertaining them in his caravan.'

'Seducing them, do you mean?'

'There've been no complaints, sir. Certainly no evidence that he's defiled girls under the age of consent.'

'I still don't like the sound of him. Why haven't you interviewed him?'

'As I mentioned, sir, I only received this information as I was leaving the station to come and report to you. I intend to pay him a visit as soon as I get back.'

The chief constable blew out a cloud of smoke, having at last got his pipe going.

'Good. I suppose you learnt all this from Atherly?'

'Yes, sir. He says he didn't come forward earlier as he was frightened.'

'Do you believe that?'

'Could be true. He's only eighteen.'

'And Price, how old is he?'

'Twenty-six.'

'Well, you'd better be on your way. Continue to report to me directly. I've promised Mr Thurston I'll keep a personal eye on things. A number of the boys at Warren Hall have fathers in important positions.'

Stadden, who had left school at the age of fourteen, accepted that boys at private boarding schools had been born with silver spoons in their mouths. But he had never felt overawed by the class distinctions that divided society at that time. He wasn't even resentful of a chief constable who hadn't long since retired from the regular army in the rank of colonel and who owed his appointment to knowing the right people.

'As a matter of fact,' the chief constable went on, 'I'm dining at Greenborough Court this evening. The Cuckfield boy is a pupil at Warren Hall.'

'I've met him, sir. He has a funny first name.'

'Denzil? It's a family name.'

'I've never come across it before.'

'Very important to maintain family traditions, Stadden. They are what has kept England and the Empire in front of the rest of the world.'

'I'm sure you're right, sir.'

'No doubt about it. Anyway, it's time you went off to put the fear of God into that nasty bit of work who lives in a caravan. The very idea of his asking Willett to show him his naked backside. And for money, too! Not only disgusting, but extremely suspicious.'

Wally Price was about to go out for the evening when Inspector Stadden, accompanied by a constable named Vicary, knocked on the door of his caravan. He had never seen either of them before, but could tell from their demeanour that this was no social visit.

'What can I do for you gents?' he enquired with a nervous smile.

'We're police officers and want to have a word with you,' Stadden said.

'If it's about Mary Froggett, I've never touched the girl. She's not my type.'

'Why do you mention her?' Stadden asked. He was standing on the top step of four that gave access to the caravan and peered past Price into the interior.

'Because I've heard she's trying to decide who to pin the blame on for getting her in the family way. It's definitely not me.'

The two men were standing almost nose to nose while PC Vicary remained at the foot of the steps. Price was freshly shaved and his hair was slicked back and held down by a surfeit of brilliantine. He was wearing a shirt and tie and his shoes positively shone.

'Going out, are you?' Stadden said.

'I'm courting a girl in the village. Norma Kirk.'

'I understand you do jobs up at Warren Hall School?'

'S'right.'

'Got to know some of the boys, have you?'

Wally Price frowned. 'I only speak when I'm spoken to. Haven't got much in common with kids at posh schools.'

'Know a boy named Willett?'

'Don't really know any of their names.'

'But you've heard of Willett?'

'Not as I recall. What's he look like?'

'When did you last do a job at the school?'

'About a week ago. They wanted a tree cut up.'

'Who did you speak to on that occasion?'

'What is this? What are you getting at?'

'Did you speak to any of the boys?'

'Can't rightly remember.'

'Try. It's important.'

'I believe a boy did come over.'

'Was he a boy who'd recently been caned by the headmaster?'

'Now you mention it, I believe he had been,' Price said uncomfortably.

16

'Did you offer him money to show you the marks on his backside?'

'I'm not interested in boys' backsides.' His tone was indignant. 'I can give you the names of half a dozen girls who'll tell you I'm absolutely normal. I'm not a homo if that's what you're suggesting.' In a suddenly suspicious voice he went on, 'Have you been talking to Joe Atherly?'

'Why do you ask?'

''Cos I remember now, he was there to help me with the tree, and this boy – Willett did you say his name was? – was with him. Joe mentioned the boy had had a caning and was showing off the marks for sixpence a look and was I interested? I told him I wasn't and soon after that the boy went off.' He shook his head slowly from side to side. 'Bloody cheek I call it. Joe Atherly had better watch his tongue.'

'I'd like to have a look round your caravan,' Stadden said. 'Any objections?'

Price hesitated, then said with a shrug, 'Not much good objecting, is it? But you won't find anything here.' He glanced at his watch. 'I'm meeting my young lady in ten minutes.'

'Where?'

'At her place. My motorcycle's round the back.'

Twenty minutes later the two officers departed. A thorough search of the caravan had failed to reveal anything of significance. Wally Price's preparations for his assignation with Norma Kirk had left his home on wheels smelling like a boiled sweet factory. Stadden was still wrinkling his nose in distaste as they walked back to their car.

'I've not finished with him yet,' he remarked grimly as they drove off.

5

The breakthrough came a few days later when some of Stephen Willett's clothing was found carefully hidden in undergrowth not far from Price's caravan.

The discovery was made by a dog named Brewster when out for

17

his morning walk. Brewster, an elderly Bassett hound, was wont to roam about in a leisurely way, returning every so often to his master's side. On one of these occasions his master noticed that he was carrying something in his mouth. The something proved to be a boy's jersey, trimmed with the blue and yellow colours of Warren Hall School. It was some while, however, before Brewster could be persuaded to show his master where he had made his find. Eventually he did so by leading the way to a ditch which was heavily overgrown with weeds. Slithering down somewhat inelegantly, the dog began digging among the tufted grass. When he withdrew his head he had in his mouth a pair of dark grey flannel shorts such as the boys of Warren Hall wore in the summer term.

His master, who lived locally and had heard about the missing boy, decided it was time to cut short their walk and return home to report their discovery.

'It's Willett's clothing all right, sir,' Stadden said. 'It has his name tapes sewn on to prove it.'

'That's conclusive enough,' the chief constable observed with a judicial nod when told of the latest developments. 'It confirms that he was dressed when he left the dormitory. In other words, he had got dressed to go out.'

'We'd already deduced that, sir.'

'I dare say, but this is proof positive. It means he must have gone to meet someone. No question of his having been abducted.'

'There never was any evidence of that, sir,' Stadden said patiently. 'If you ask me, he went to meet Price.'

'It's near enough two miles from the school to Price's caravan.'

'It's my guess that Price met him with his motorcycle.

'Can't you find a witness who saw them together?' the chief constable asked as if it were a question of looking behind trees.

'I doubt if we'll be able to do that. It's likely it all happened before anyone was up and about.'

The chief constable puffed thoughtfully at his pipe. Through a cloud of smoke he said abruptly, 'And motive, Stadden, what about motive?'

'Price is a pervert, sir. Because he goes with girls doesn't mean he can't fancy boys. Young boys of Willett's age.'

18

The chief constable pulled a face. 'No real proof of that.'

'Don't forget, sir, that he offered Willett money to expose his bare backside. Seems pretty compelling evidence to me, though he denied it, of course.'

'Why should Willett have agreed to go off with this nasty piece of work?'

'I've thought a lot about that, sir. It seems Willett was something of a loner. He didn't have any close friends at the school. He didn't enjoy games like cricket and football and he didn't excel in the classroom. My enquiries show that it was much the same during the school holidays which he spent with his grandfather in Shropshire. Most days he'd apparently wander off on his own and only come back to the house at meal-times.' Stadden paused. 'I gather the staff are all elderly, so it's not surprising that young Willett was left to his own devices. He didn't give them any trouble and they didn't interfere in his comings and goings.'

There was a knock on the door and an officer entered.

'I thought you'd want to know this immediately, sir,' he said. 'Blood stains have been found on Willett's jersey.'

The chief constable glanced at Stadden. 'Perhaps we're getting somewhere,' he said.

6

It was four months later on a grey November morning, with mist hanging low over the fields and hedgerows, that Walter Price pleaded not guilty to the charge of murdering Stephen Willett. The oak-panelled assize court had been the scene of numerous murder trials during the hundred years since it was built. It was a gloomy chamber in which only the judge in his scarlet robe provided any colour. There were still gas brackets on the walls which had been in use until just after World War I when electricity took over.

The trial was being held before Mr Justice Gurdon, a senior judge of the King's Bench Division whose austere demeanour added to the solemnity of the scene. He was noted neither for his leniency nor for displaying any emotion when passing sentence of death on a prisoner convicted of murder. Everyone was aware that should Price be convicted, he would certainly be hanged. The Home Secretary rarely found any grounds for recommending reprieves in cases where children had been the victims of murder.

. As for Wally Price, public opinion had shown itself solidly against him. To the populace at large he was not only a murderer, but one who had acted from motives of lust and depravity.

Newspapers had carried articles by legal experts explaining the circumstances in which a person could still be found guilty of murder even though a body had never been discovered.

This, of course, was the fundamental weakness of the crown's case, for Stephen Willett's body had never been found, despite vast tracts of land having been dug up, as well as ponds and rivers being dredged to no avail. There were few people, however, who didn't believe he had been killed and his body cunningly disposed of.

Nevertheless Price had maintained his innocence throughout numerous interrogations. 'If there's a God,' he said on more than one occasion, 'He'll not let me hang.'

The court was packed when Mr Justice Gurdon took his seat on the first day of the trial. The representatives of the press overflowed their allotted space and there was a full turn-out by the wives of the county's dignitaries to whom a murder trial had a frisson all of its own, particularly if it ended in a sentence of death.

After the jury had been sworn in, Mr Marcus Lovesey opened the case for the crown. He told the jury it was an irresistible inference that eleven-year-old Stephen Willett was dead and that once that was accepted, everything pointed to the accused having killed him. The boy's school jersey had been found hidden in undergrowth. Moreover, it bore bloodstains of the same blood group as that of the accused man. It had to be conceded, however, that it was the most common blood group of all and that unfortunately the boy's own blood group was unknown.

Mr Lovesey concluded his opening speech and was followed by a succession of witnesses giving the testimony to which they had already deposed in the magistrates' court. This, with their cross-examination, occupied the whole of the first day, leaving the crown's case complete apart from the evidence of Inspector Stadden who went into the witness-box first thing the next morning.

As he stepped down from the box, the judge, who had scarcely said a word, turned to defence counsel and asked him if he had a submission to make. Mr Fergus Anderson KC, who was leading for the defence, needed no second bidding and proceeded to submit that his client had no case to answer: that is to say, that the crown had failed to produce sufficient evidence to justify requiring the accused to put forward his defence. Mr Lovesey replied to the submission. Then Mr Justice Gurdon turned to the jury and addressed them in a voice that sounded like dry leaves rustling on a marble floor.

'Members of the jury, every murder charge requires, amongst other evidence, proof of a dead body. In this case that would mean proof that eleven-year-old Stephen Willett is conclusively dead. Obviously the absence of a body makes such proof that much more difficult. Suspicion is not enough, for no amount of suspicion can ever amount to proof. Having listened very carefully to the evidence put before you by the crown, I have to tell you that it is not sufficient to support a prima-facie case of murder. I therefore direct you as a matter of law to find the accused not guilty of the charge.'

Wally Price clutched the iron rail which ran along the front edge of the dock and glanced up at the ceiling as if in thanks to the Almighty for his deliverance. To many in court, however, it was a moment of intense anti-climax.

Subsequently he returned to Greenborough and went to live with his elderly parents. His caravan had been sold while he was in prison awaiting trial.

A number of villagers regarded his resumption of life in their midst as a gross affront, but others, mostly younger ones, argued that he had been tried and acquitted and was entitled to be treated as an innocent person.

Though the school never employed him again, he managed to earn a sufficient living, until one morning about six months later when he blew his brains out with his father's shotgun.

'Proves he killed the boy, but couldn't live any longer with his conscience,' said half the village, with an exchange of knowing glances.

Nothing further was ever heard of Stephen Willett. Warren Hall weathered the scandal, while Stephen's mother grieved for a son she felt she had scarcely known.

PART II

PART II

1

On the evidence of the first six months of the new decade, Rosa Epton saw little chance of it emulating the naughty nineties of the previous century. Everyone was suddenly far too busy worrying about the shrinking ozone layer and the destruction of rain forests to have time to be frivolous or naughty.

Moreover, nineteen ninety had begun badly for Rosa personally. In January she had sprained her ankle severely on the first day of a Swiss skiing holiday, which had left her limping about the hotel on a stick and watching others streaking down the slopes. Peter Chen, who was with her and who was an excellent skier, did his best to cheer her up in the evenings, but was only partially successful. Rosa had been for returning home immediately and leaving Peter to enjoy himself. He had said firmly, however, that either they both stayed or both came home.

'After all,' he had added, 'you're still able to enjoy the *après-ski*.'

'If you mean drinking, it's about all I can do,' Rosa had replied.

Then a few weeks after they got back, Rosa had her car stolen from outside her flat. It was later found abandoned in south London with all its removable objects removed.

Finally, around Easter, Robin Snaith, her senior partner in Snaith and Epton, was rushed into hospital for an emergency appendicectomy, which left Rosa to run the office on her own for a month.

Telling herself that bad breaks went in threes and that the first half of the year had now passed, she was hoping the second six months would be trouble-free by comparison.

'Your godmother has surfaced again,' Stephanie said when Rosa returned from court one morning in early July.

'Not here in the office?' Rosa said in some alarm.

'No, there's a letter from her. I recognised her flamboyant handwriting,' Stephanie replied with a faint smile.

Stephanie, who was Snaith and Epton's telephonist-cum-receptionist, knew more about what went on in the office than anyone else. The only time things teetered on the brink of collapse was when she was away. She and Rosa had always enjoyed a special rapport.

She now went on, 'You were saying only the other day that you'd not heard from her since she sold her flat at Deepwood Grange and were wondering what had happened to her.'

Rosa nodded, 'Did you notice the postmark on the letter, Steph?'

'It was smudged,' Stephanie replied with a small sardonic smile.

'Oh, well, at least she's still alive.'

Aunt Margaret had been out of Rosa's life from the time she was an adolescent until a few years previously when she suddenly popped up as Margaret Lakington, thrice married and thrice widowed. Each of her husbands had left her well enough off to have no financial problems and when Rosa had gone to stay with her, she had said she was ready to settle down. After a lifetime of living abroad, she had put travelling behind her. But events at Deepwood Grange had caused her to change her mind and the last Rosa had heard of her was almost a year ago when she announced that she had put her flat on the market and was planning to take a leisurely cruise. Rosa had replied, wishing her well and telling her to beware of fortune hunters. Her godmother had written back thanking her for her good wishes and saying that she had had more practice than most in seeing off fortune hunters and that, anyway, she was now nearly eighty. To Rosa, however, that only made her even more desirable prey.

She reached her office and sat down at her desk. Margaret Lakington's letter was on top of the pile. Her somewhat ornamental handwriting was, indeed, unmistakable: the postmark, as Stephanie had said, indecipherable. She slit open the envelope and extracted two sheets of folded paper. Glancing first at the end she let out a small groan for it was signed not Margaret Lakington but Margaret Pickard.

'Surely she can't have married a fourth husband,' Rosa exclaimed to her empty office.

She turned back to the first page to find out the address. 'The Post Office, Greenborough' was all that appeared. Perhaps it was an accommodation address. There was only one thing to do; read the letter and hope that all would become clear.

Dear Rosa, [it began]

I never intended being out of touch for so long, but dipping in and out of your life seems to have become a feature of my own. Anyway, here I am, a sub-postmistress of all unlikely occupations, though in my case the title is entirely honorific. It is Adrian who has become a real live postmaster. An adjoining cottage where we live is part of the deal. I should explain that I met Adrian Pickard on a cruise and we immediately hit it off. He was on the entertainment staff, being an accomplished pianist and singer of all those Noël Coward and Cole Porter songs that never seem to lose popularity. Shortly before the cruise ended he proposed and we got married at Brighton Registry Office as soon as arrangements could be made. Adrian was keen that we should keep it entirely private, which is my excuse for not letting you know. We moved here about six weeks ago and everything seems to be working out well. Greenborough is a most attractive village and relatively unspoilt, and London is only an hour's drive away. There's still a lord of the manor at Greenborough Court and one of those boys' prep schools with dynastic pretensions.

But the purpose of this letter is to renew contact and suggest that you come down for Sunday lunch in the near future. Cooking is another of Adrian's accomplishments. Do write and say you'll come. I say write because I still have an aversion toward the telephone, save in dire necessity.

Your errant but ever affectionate godmother,
Margaret Pickard.

P.S. Adrian bears no resemblance to a fortune hunter! I know you'll be wondering how old he is, so I had better tell you – forty-two. You see I can almost read your thoughts from here.

Rosa put down the letter and sighed. The postscript did little to reassure her. It was difficult to see anything but waywardness in marrying for a fourth time when you were almost eighty. A man, moreover, who was near enough half her age. A pianist on a cruise liner who had wanted to be a postmaster. It was too bizarre for words.

Reaching into a drawer of her desk she pulled out a sheet of writing paper and composed an immediate reply.

Dear Margaret,
I was delighted to get your letter and should love to come down for lunch one Sunday. I'm so glad you're happy and well and I look forward to meeting Adrian.
Much love,
Rosa.

As she read the letter through, she realised that to say she was looking forward to meeting Adrian amounted to the understatement of the year. She had seldom felt more agog at the prospect of an encounter.

2

Two and a half weeks later Rosa set off one Sunday morning for Greenborough in her small Honda. By the time she had shaken off London's outer suburbs she was halfway there. It was a sunny but breezy day with white clouds scudding across a blue sky.

Margaret had said she couldn't possibly miss the post office, which proved to be true. It was not only plainly labelled, but had a freshly painted red pillar box outside to draw attention to itself. Its window was full of practical items such as ballpoint pens and children's colouring books. A notice proclaimed that it also sold 'High Class Confectionery'. Tacked on to one end of the post office was a low, thatched cottage with a small front garden. As she was taking all this in she became aware of Margaret gesticulating at her from a downstairs window. A moment later the front door opened and her godmother appeared.

'Rosa, dear!' she called out. 'Leave your car where it is and come in.'

In the time since Rosa had last seen her Margaret appeared unchanged apart from a few more lines on her face. She had on one of the wide-brimmed hats she had begun wearing at the time she took to a wig and it perfectly suited her tall, willowy figure. She had only once referred to her headgear, and then in an offhand tone. It seemed that an illness had caused her hair to fall out and ever since she had worn a wig. As Rosa recalled, she would wear a hat all day and only take it off at dinner time.

Rosa got out of the car and hurried to greet her godmother with a careful kiss on the cheek. She knew Margaret didn't like effusive physical contact.

'How lovely to see you again, Rosa! This must be the last place on earth you ever thought I'd end up. Living next to a post office, I mean.'

'Your letter certainly came as a surprise,' Rosa said with a smile. 'How did you find it?'

'Adrian saw it advertised and immediately said it was a must for us. He'd always longed to run a post office rather in the way boys used to want to become engine drivers. We came and looked at the property and soon reached an agreement with the previous occupant and the postal authorities to buy it. I think it helped that I offered to renovate the cottage at my own expense.' She gave a shrug. 'Why not? After all it was going to be our home.'

'How has the village reacted to having such an unconventional postmistress?' Rosa asked.

Margaret gave a quick throaty laugh. 'Most of the locals have taken our arrival in their stride. Only the uppercrust are slightly put out and not sure if we're real. Sir Denzil Cuckfield who lives at Greenborough Court came into the post office the first week we were here and hasn't appeared again since after finding me behind the counter. He probably now sends to Harrods for his postage stamps. On the other hand his wife is a dear and always ready to pass the time of day.'

'Isn't there a junior minister in the government with the name of Cuckfield?'

'Martin Cuckfield; he's their son. Very up and coming, I'm told. He has a constituency somewhere in the Midlands.'

'I take it you're not on visiting terms with the Cuckfields?'

'Good gracious, no. We maintain friendly relations with the village, but remain socially aloof.' She paused and gazed toward the front door of the cottage. 'Adrian and I have no wish to be caught up in a lot of social activity. We're more than happy in one another's company. We're ready to give the village our moral support, but that's about the limit of our involvement.'

'Hasn't the vicar tried to draw you into parish events?' Rosa asked with a touch of mischief, recalling her godmother's somewhat caustic views on the work of the church.

'As a matter of fact he and Adrian get on rather well. Adrian has helped out by playing the organ when the regular organist hasn't been available. Mrs Timms, the vicar's wife, is a thoroughly worthy lady and likes to drop in for a cup of morning coffee when she's in the vicinity.' Leading the way into the cottage she called out to her husband in her deep husky voice. 'Rosa's here. Leave the kitchen and come and show yourself.'

A moment later a figure appeared at the end of the passage. He was wearing a butcher's apron and came forward with an uneasy smile on his face as if aware he was under a microscope.

'How nice to meet you, Rosa! I've heard so much about you.' He shook her hand, then leaned forward and gave her a quick kiss on the cheek. Turning to his wife, he said, 'Let me get you and Rosa a drink and then I must return to the kitchen.' Glancing at Rosa he went on, 'I love cooking, so it's no penance. But we're starting with a cheese soufflé and they're apt to be temperamental, as I'm sure you know.'

'I'm afraid I'm a very basic cook,' Rosa said. 'My flights of fancy in the kitchen usually end in disaster.'

'Well?' Margaret asked as soon as her husband had poured them drinks and retreated to the kitchen.

'Well, what?'

'You know perfectly well what I mean. What's your impression of Adrian?'

'First impression entirely favourable,' Rosa replied, a trifle embarrassed.

Her impression had, in fact, been of a sun-tanned, even-featured, well-preserved man of middle years. What still remained a mystery, however, was the chemical mix that had brought him and Margaret to the altar. Or, more accurately, before Brighton's registrar of marriages.

'I felt sure you'd like each other,' Margaret said, sipping her glass of sherry. 'You don't think I'm mad, do you?'

'Of course I don't. I'm delighted you're happy.'

'I know he looks young enough to be my son, but I can't begin to tell you what fun we have together. Companionship is the name of the game.' Holding out her glass she said, 'Pour me another sherry and get yourself another drink. What is it Adrian's given you?'

'Campari soda, but one's enough in the middle of the day. I must stay sober for the drive home.'

'Well, we'll fill you up with black coffee, if need be. Anyway, don't talk about going home when you've hardly arrived. Now, what was I saying?'

'That you and Adrian enjoyed an excellent companionship.'

'That's right, we do.' She looked up and caught Rosa's gaze. 'After four husbands, I should know how to handle men.'

Rosa smiled, but doubted the necessary logic of this.

'And what about you?' her godmother went on. 'Isn't it time you got married? Do you still have a relationship with that nice young Chinese lawyer?'

'Peter Chen? Yes, we still see each other.'

'That could mean anything,' Margaret said crisply.

'All right, we're still having a relationship.'

'Might you marry him?'

'He'd like that, but I'm less sure it's a good idea. Anyway, I don't want to marry anyone at the moment. Peter and I are very fond of each other and maybe one day . . .'

'Why didn't you bring him with you today?'

'He's in New York for a week. But even if he hadn't been, I'd decided I'd sooner come on my own.'

At that moment Adrian appeared in the doorway to announce that lunch was ready.

'We modernised and extended the kitchen to include a dining area,' Margaret said as they set off down the passage to the rear of the cottage. 'It was positively medieval before and Adrian designed it afresh.'

'Do you do any cooking at all these days?' Rosa enquired of her godmother.

31

'I occasionally make a piece of toast and boil a kettle, but you know I was never any use in the kitchen. Living abroad most of my life, there were always servants to wait on one.'

The dining area was entirely glass on one side, overlooking a garden of unmown grass and fruit trees.

'Very rustic,' Rosa observed.

'Adrian wants to turn it into a vegetable garden,' Margaret said, 'but I'm all for leaving it as it is. We can buy fresh vegetables in the village. No point in growing our own.'

Adrian smiled, but said nothing.

The meal was delicious, the cheese soufflé being followed by poached salmon accompanied by a home-made hollandaise sauce, together with new potatoes and thinly sliced cucumber in mint flavoured vinegar. Finally, there was a fresh fruit salad.

During the course of lunch, Margaret and Adrian took turns in regaling Rosa with stories of the cruise on which they had met.

'How many cruises have you been on?' Rosa asked, addressing Adrian.

'Over a dozen. Some were better than others, but I'm not sorry to have hung up my lifebelt. If I ever go on another, it'll be as a passenger.'

'Being a village postmaster must be about as far as you can get from entertaining passengers on a cruise ship.'

'I hadn't thought of it like that, but I suppose it is. A very refreshing change, I may say.' He glanced at his wife. 'It's all thanks to Margaret, who has helped me realise an ambition.'

It still struck Rosa as a curious ambition, but she refrained from saying so. On the other hand she could see that, after years spent at sea, there were attractions in settling down in the English countryside.

'I imagine that a village post office is the clearing house for all the local gossip,' she remarked.

'My two assistants always seem to be aware of everything that's going on. I don't know if Margaret's told you, two village ladies help out in the post office. Mrs Ives, otherwise Ivy, and Mrs Cassidy who is known to one and all as Betty. I couldn't run it without them. They know everyone and everything.'

'I'm only called upon in an emergency,' Margaret interjected. 'Like when Mrs Ives' son went down with measles and Mrs Cassidy's husband fell off a ladder, both on the same day.'

'Life here has a good solid feel to it,' Adrian went on. 'I believe Margaret has mentioned the Cuckfields. They've lived at Greenborough Court for generations. Sir Denzil may be an old reactionary, but his family provide an air of stability. Then there's Warren Hall School. The present headmaster is the third generation Thurston to run it and there's an old chap and his wife who live in a cottage on the edge of the school grounds who've lived in Greenborough all their lives.'

'Do I know them?' Margaret enquired.

'He comes into the post office to collect their pensions each week and to buy his favourite brand of tobacco which we keep in stock specially for him. His wife suffers from arthritis and doesn't get out much.'

'You've told us everything about them, except their name,' Margaret observed sardonically.

'Joe and Gwen Atherly,' Adrian said with an apologetic smile. He pushed back his chair. 'Take Rosa back into the front room and I'll bring you coffee.'

'Let me help clear the table,' Rosa said.

'Absolutely not,' her hosts said in unison.

Rosa followed her godmother out of the kitchen. As they sat waiting for the coffee to come, Margaret said, 'There's a reason for Adrian harping on about stable backgrounds and dynastic ties. It's because he's lacked them in his own life. He never knew his mother. She upped and left her husband for a GI soon after Adrian's birth. She was last heard of in Arkansas, after which she sank from sight. His father did his best to bring Adrian up and then he was killed in a car accident when Adrian was only ten. For the next six years of his life he was shunted from one set of foster parents to another, until at the age of sixteen he decided to make his own way in the world.' She sighed. 'Is it any wonder the poor man longs for some stability in his life? Marrying me has helped, I'm glad to say.' She turned her head. 'Ah, here's the coffee.'

'Why don't I show Rosa the garden?' Adrian said some twenty minutes later when they had finished.

'She's already seen it through the kitchen window,' Margaret remarked.

'That's not the same as stepping outside.'

'If you want to show her something, I suggest you walk round the village.'

33

'I'd like that,' Rosa said quickly. 'And you can have your siesta, Margaret.'

'I don't have one when we're entertaining guests,' Margaret said, smothering a yawn.

'Go on, put your feet up and close your eyes,' Adrian said, placing a cushion behind her head. 'We won't be gone long.'

'I can see she's lost none of her stubbornness,' Rosa said as she and Adrian walked down the front path.

'The day she does will be the day to alert the undertaker,' Adrian said with a laugh. They reached the footpath. 'We'll go this way and I can show you the major sights – the local pub and the entrance to Greenborough Court. You can't see the house at this time of year because of the trees, but once they've shed their leaves it's visible from the road. I drove up to it soon after we arrived to deliver a registered parcel to Lady Cuckfield. It wasn't really my job, but I thought it would earn me a merit point.'

'And did it?'

'I guess so. She phoned later to thank me for my trouble.' After a pause, he went on in a slightly embarrassed voice, 'I wanted an opportunity to speak to you on your own, Rosa. In particular I want to say that the very last thing I intend is to come between Margaret and her family and friends. I certainly hope that you'll be a frequent visitor and keep in close touch with her. She never seems to have made friends easily and now most of her acquaintances are dead. She corresponds intermittently with a sister-in-law who lives in South Africa and that's about all.'

'Would that be Ted Lakington's sister?'

'Yes.'

A silence fell between them. Eventually Rosa said, 'My only concern is that you should be happy together. I can see that the age difference might present problems, but you obviously thought that out before you got married.'

'I'm only conscious of it when other people are. I've grown used to surprised looks and awkward silences. I don't need to tell you what a wonderful companion Margaret can be.'

'You must have met a good many interesting people in your job.'

'A lot of very nice ones and also a great many horrendously awful ones.'

They had reached the end of the main village street and Adrian

34

suggested they should turn back. On their return they found Margaret standing over a kettle in the kitchen.

'I thought I'd greet you with a cup of tea,' she said.

'After which I ought to make tracks for London,' Rosa remarked.

'Next time you come you must bring Peter. I'm sure he and Adrian will get on. Adrian's been to Singapore a number of times.'

'Peter's from Hong Kong.'

Margaret made an imperious gesture. 'They're both full of Chinese. Anyway, he's been there too.' She began pouring boiling water into the teapot and said suddenly, 'I've had a brainwave. Why don't you and Peter come down for our village fête in two weeks time? It's being held in the grounds of Greenborough Court and being opened by the Cuckfields' MP son. It's believed, though heaven knows why, that having a member of parliament present will bring in the crowds.'

'I'll have a word with Peter when he gets back and let you know,' Rosa said.

'We'll have lunch here first and then Adrian can drive us to the fête. He's promised to play an ancient barrel-organ to raise funds for the church. Tell Peter it's a chance in a lifetime to participate in a piece of village ritual.'

Rosa refrained from pointing out that Peter had probably attended more English village fêtes than her godmother. He had been educated in England and had conscientiously immersed himself in the mores of the country of his adoption.

As she drove back to London that Sunday afternoon, Rosa reflected on her visit. She had enjoyed seeing Margaret again and the eagerly awaited encounter with her new husband had passed off without any hint of drama. She wasn't too sure what she had expected, other than some sort of atmospheric crackling. But Adrian had behaved impeccably throughout and had gone out of his way to allay any doubts she might have had about him. It could hardly be called a love match; even so there didn't appear to be anything sinister about their surprising union.

She hadn't long been home when her telephone rang.

'It's me,' Peter Chen said, his voice as clear as if he were sitting

35

at the other end of the settee. 'How was your trip to see godmother Margaret?'

'What you're really asking is, what did I think of her new husband?'

'Well?'

'He was very nice.'

'You were won over?'

'I suppose I was.'

'He could still be after her money.'

'I know, but I don't think he is. I believe it's a genuine match. It suits both of them and they seem to be very happy in each other's company.'

'Well, well.'

'You'll be able to make up your own mind about them. We've been invited down a week next Saturday. Margaret thought you'd enjoy their village fête. She assumed you'd never attended one before.'

Peter let out an exclamation. 'I, who have bought more raffle tickets, guessed the weight of more fruit cakes and failed to dislodge more immovable coconuts than any other living Chinese . . .'

Rosa laughed. 'You'd like to go, wouldn't you?'

'I'd like to go anywhere with you. I'm missing you terribly. Why don't you get on Concorde tomorrow and we can fly back together on Wednesday?'

'I've never known anyone so full of impractical suggestions,' Rosa said cheerfully. 'Anyway, I'm in court all tomorrow and the next day, so flights to New York are also flights of fancy.' She paused. 'How's your trip working out, Peter?'

'Satisfactorily. I hope to clinch the deal tomorrow.'

Peter Chen had a string of extremely wealthy clients, Hong Kong Chinese and Arabs from the Gulf States for the most part, on whose behalf he flew about the world negotiating deals worth millions of dollars, a percentage of which ended up in his own pocket as a fee. As Rosa had often reflected, they were both solicitors, though her own remuneration from her criminal practice bore no more resemblance to Peter's income than a farm worker's did to a ducal landowner's. But that didn't matter in the slightest.

'What have you been doing today?' she asked.

'Working in my hotel room.'

'Haven't you been out at all?'

'It's been too hot. Around a hundred degrees, with humidity to match.'

'What are you going to do this evening?'

'Lie on my bed and think of you.'

'That doesn't sound very imaginative.'

'You'd be surprised what my imagination can get up to.'

Shortly after this, they had a final exchange of endearments and then disconnected.

Rosa was looking forward eagerly to Peter's return. In a sudden burst of optimism she felt that her year was definitely going to get better.

3

When Peter arrived to pick Rosa up on the day of the Greenborough fête, the first thing she noticed as she got into the car was a huge bouquet of cellophane-wrapped roses on the back seat.

'Are those for Margaret?' she asked as she fastened her seat belt.

He shook his head. 'Old Chinese custom,' he replied in a sing-song voice, 'sweet-smelling flowers for new husband of old wife.'

Rosa gave him a patient smile. 'They're beautiful, Peter. I know Margaret will be delighted.'

'That's the idea.'

She enjoyed being driven by Peter and always felt completely safe. He had recently bought a new BMW which had more gadgets than a mad scientist could have invented. For all that, she was still devoted to her own small car which had fewer things to go wrong with it.

'I've also come properly equipped for the afternoon,' he said, nodding at a small bag resting in a tray between their seats.

Rosa picked it up. 'It feels like money.'

'It is. Fifty one-pound coins. You need lots of loose change at these village fêtes.'

'That's more than loose change. It's enough to start the church clock going again.'

In considerably less time than it had taken Rosa to make the journey, they arrived in Greenborough and parked outside the post office. The scene was more hectic than it had been on Rosa's Sunday visit. People were mailing letters and to-ing and fro-ing with the purposefulness of a colony of ants. She could see Adrian's head above the barricade of stationery that filled the window.

Taking Peter's arm she led the way to the front door of the cottage. Before she could ring the bell, the door was flung open to reveal Margaret in an actressy pose.

After accepting a kiss from Rosa, she offered her cheek to her companion. 'How nice to see you again, Peter.'

'These are for you, Mrs Pickard,' he said, handing over the flowers.

'Aren't they gorgeous?' Margaret exclaimed with genuine delight. 'A gentleman giving a lady flowers is one of the few touches of gallantry to have survived in our egalitarian age. Now come on in. Adrian will be back soon and then we'll have lunch. I'm afraid it's all a bit of a rush, but the fête starts at two and Adrian feels we ought to be there to hear Martin Cuckfield open it.' She gave an expressive shrug. 'I can't think why, but I suppose we mustn't let the postmaster down.' She smiled. 'Dear Adrian, he's taking his job so seriously, I've said I'll have to design him a special uniform. But the great thing is he's enjoying himself.'

Lunch (a cold collation and salad, followed by a selection of cheeses) passed off agreeably and shortly before two o'clock Adrian said it was time to leave.

'You can take Rosa in the Volvo,' Margaret announced, 'and I shall go with Peter in his new BMW. That'll set the tongues wagging.'

As for years past, the fête was being held in a large open field which was separated from the main lawns and flowerbeds by a well-trimmed yew hedge. All points of access to the house and its surrounding garden carried signs saying, 'Strictly Private. Keep Out'.

'Typical,' Margaret said with an indignant snort as she led Rosa to a gap in the hedge to get a better view of Greenborough Court.

'I can see they wouldn't want people trampling over the garden and peering through their windows,' Rosa said pacifically.

'Local villagers are not the same as football hooligans,' Margaret observed in a scornful tone. She glanced up at a small group of people approaching the gap where they were standing. 'Here are the Cuckfields coming now. That's Sir Denzil on the right talking to the chairman of the Parochial Church Council.'

Lady Cuckfield and her son were just behind and she greeted Margaret with a friendly smile.

'Aren't we lucky with the weather, Mrs Pickard?' she said.

'Indeed, yes,' Margaret replied. She continued quickly, 'Let me introduce my goddaughter, Rosa, who's a solicitor in London. Lady Cuckfield, Rosa Epton.'

'Oh, you must meet my son. He was called to the Bar before he entered politics.'

Martin Cuckfield had walked ahead and had caught up with his father and the chairman of the Parochial Church Council as they reached a small dais with a striped canopy drooping over it.

'Joyce,' Sir Denzil bellowed back at his wife.

'I'd better go,' Lady Cuckfield said, 'I'll look forward to seeing you later.'

'She's a nice woman,' Margaret observed. 'It can't be much fun being married to Sir D. He may have been born a gentleman, but he has few of the natural instincts. Though I grant you he's a handsome beast. Let's go nearer and hear which platitudes Martin is going to share with us.'

A minute or so later, the voice of the chairman of the Parochial Church Council crackled out from loudspeakers hung on trees and strategically placed poles.

' . . . Great privilege . . . indebted to Sir Denzil and Lady Cuckfield for their generosity in lending their field for our annual fête . . . great honour to introduce Mr Martin Cuckfield who has so kindly agreed to open the fête . . . MP, junior minister in the government and one of Greenborough's sons of which it can be truly proud . . . without more ado, let me introduce Mr Martin Cuckfield.'

He stepped back from the microphone to scattered applause and Martin Cuckfield took his place. Despite a slightly effete appearance, his voice was strong and confident. Rosa reckoned he was around forty, maybe still in his thirties.

He spoke with pride at having been born in Greenborough and at growing up in the village. Worship in its church was, it seemed, a particularly cherished memory.

'You've come here primarily to spend your money and I mustn't keep you from that worthy purpose,' he went on. 'Indeed, I urge you to throw thrift to the winds and to spend freely in an excellent cause. Village fêtes are the stuff of which England is made. They represent life at its best, enshrining as they do, the traditions which bind us together . . .'

'Dear God!' Margaret murmured in Rosa's ear. 'You can almost hear the gas escaping.'

'It therefore gives me very great pleasure to declare the fête open. I wish you all an enjoyable free-spending time.' As he finished to a quickly dying round of polite applause, Peter came up beside Margaret and Rosa.

'Where's Adrian?' Margaret asked.

'Talking to a man over there.'

'I don't think I've ever seen him before. They seem to be having a very animated conversation. I wonder who he is.'

The person in question had greying hair and gesticulated a lot. He was laughing and frequently paused to wave to people passing by. Eventually, he and Adrian disengaged and Adrian came over to where they were standing.

'Who was that you were talking to?' Margaret enquired.

'Mr Thurston. He's the headmaster of Warren Hall School, as were his father and grandfather before him. He seems a very genuine sort of person. I've offered to give them a piano recital if they'd like.'

'It seems social barriers are breaking down all round,' Margaret remarked. Turning to Rosa she added, 'We're obviously not as socially aloof as I suggested the last time you were here.'

A voice spoke behind them. 'Mrs Pickard, let me introduce my son, Martin. And this is Mrs Pickard's goddaughter who's a solicitor, Miss Epton.'

'And I'm a solicitor, too,' Peter chimed in. 'And a friend of Rosa's.'

Martin Cuckfield shook hands all round. 'What fun these occasions are,' he said unconvincingly.

'I always imagine,' Rosa said, 'that members of parliament spend all their Saturdays attending fêtes in aid of one good cause or another.'

'Pretty well,' Cuckfield said with a smile. 'Actually there's one in my constituency today and my wife is standing in for me.'

'Poor Martin is pursued by official papers wherever he goes,' Lady Cuckfield said in an aside to Rosa. 'I'm hoping he'll get promotion in the next reshuffle. He'll have earned it.'

'Mother, what are you saying?' her son asked sharply.

'Nothing, dear.'

'Oh, there you both are,' boomed Sir Denzil, approaching from the other side. 'I want you to come and meet Canon Gates, Martin. He'd like to talk to you about recent episcopal appointments.'

'About which I know nothing.'

'Doesn't matter, come and meet him.' Glancing at his wife, he added, 'After that I'm going back to the house for a cup of tea.'

'There's a tea tent over there, dear,' Lady Cuckfield said in her diffident way.

'I'm well aware of it,' her husband retorted and stalked off taking his son with him.

'He's positively boorish,' Margaret remarked, after Lady Cuckfield had drifted away in another direction. 'It's fortunate that Martin seems to take more after his mother than his father.'

'You see that old chap over there by the tombola?' Adrian said.

'Yes. What are you going to tell us about him?'

'He's Joe Atherly. He began working at the school when he was sixteen and was there at the time of the great scandal in the early thirties.'

'What was that about?' Rosa enquired.

'It wasn't so much a scandal as a tragic drama. A boy disappeared and was never heard of again. A local man was charged with murder, but was acquitted.'

'How could he have been charged if the boy's body was never found?' Margaret asked.

'If there's conclusive evidence that the victim is dead, you don't need a body,' Rosa said. 'There was a famous case involving a passenger on a Union Castle liner whose body was never found and a steward who was convicted of her murder.

It was known as the port-hole murder, which tells you what happened.'

'You've not mentioned this before,' Margaret said to her husband in an accusing tone.

'I only heard about it the other day,' Adrian said brusquely. 'Somebody in the post office was saying that Joe Atherly could probably sell his story to a Sunday newspaper. Interest in unsolved mysteries never really dies away. Incidentally, I gather Sir Denzil was a boy at the school when it happened.'

'Pity he wasn't the victim,' Margaret remarked caustically. 'Well, I suppose we'd better go and spend some money. I shall begin at the cake stall.'

'You'll be unlucky,' Peter said. 'They're always the first thing to go. But don't worry, because I've already bought two. They're being looked after by one of the kind ladies running the stall. I told her one of them was for you.'

'What a wonderful man you are!' Margaret exclaimed. Addressing Rosa she went on, 'Do you appreciate him sufficiently?'

'I can't tell you now. Too much praise goes to his head,' Rosa said.

Peter seized her hand. 'Come on, I'll win you something.'

'Anything but a goldfish.' Rosa still remembered church fêtes in the village where she had grown up and where her father had been rector. Many were the goldfish she had carefully carried home in a small, dripping plastic bag, only to discover the tiny creature mysteriously dead a few days later. The death of one particularly cherished goldfish had been her first experience of God not always answering prayers.

It was around seven o'clock when she and Peter left to drive back to London. They had returned to the Pickards' cottage two hours earlier and had slumped exhausted into comfortable chairs.

'I've really enjoyed today,' Peter remarked as they waved goodbye to their hosts and sped off in the direction of the main road. 'Britain would still have an Empire if there were more of Margaret's sort around.'

'There's always been more than a touch of the mem-sahib about her,' Rosa said. 'What did you think of Adrian?'

Peter was silent for a moment. 'Very affable and friendly,' he said at length.

'That all?'

He sighed. 'More than ever it strikes me as a crazy marriage. Your godmother must have gone a bit soft in the head, even if she does appear saner than most other people. I can only think of one reason for Adrian wanting to marry her.'

'Her money?'

'Precisely.'

'There *are* men who go for older women,' Rosa said, as if trying to convince herself. 'Margaret's always had men in her life and obviously felt the need for companionship after Ted Lakington's death. In any event, even if Adrian does have an eye on her money, it doesn't follow that he won't be a good husband to her while she lives.'

'While she lives,' Peter repeated. 'Let's hope he waits for nature to take its course.'

'You don't seriously think he'd bump her off?'

'Depends on all sorts of things. I'm only saying it's a very strange union.'

Rosa sat in silence while Peter overtook a long line of cars at a speed well in excess of the limit.

'All I can do,' she said at length, 'is to stay in touch with her and keep my eyes and ears open.'

'I agree.'

'If anything arouses my suspicions, I'll have to decide what to do.'

'That's about it,' Peter observed.

A further silence fell between them, as it often did when they were driving home after a day out.

'Is there anything you've not told me, Peter?' she said suddenly. 'You've sown a worm of doubt in my mind about Adrian Pickard.'

'I'm sure it's been there all the time. All I may have done is make it wriggle.'

'But I had the impression you got on with him.'

'I did. I've said I found him friendly, but that doesn't blind me to the facts. Namely, a forty-year-old ship's pianist marrying a wealthy widow twice his age. And then the improbable story about always having wanted to run a village post office.'

'I don't find anything sinister in that. After all they had to settle somewhere and Greenborough's a very attractive place.'

'I just wonder how long they'll stay there?'

43

'What makes you say that?'

'It was something Adrian himself said when we were in the tea tent.'

'What was that?'

'Merely that he didn't expect to spend the rest of his days there.'

'That all?'

'Yes.'

'I'd hardly expect him to contemplate staying there for the rest of his life,' Rosa said robustly.

'What about for the rest of Margaret's?' Peter enquired with a quizzical glance at the driving mirror.

4

The next evening Rosa decided to call and thank the Pickards for their hospitality. Knowing her godmother's dislike of the phone, she wasn't surprised when Adrian answered.

'Peter and I enjoyed the day very much,' she said. 'I just wanted to say thank you from both of us.'

'We enjoyed having you, Rosa. Even though it was only the second time we've met, I feel I've known you for much longer. And we both like Peter.'

'I hope Margaret's none the worse for an exhausting day.'

'She's fine. She's upstairs at the moment, but I'll get her for you if you hang on.'

'Don't bother. Just give her our love.'

'Will do. Come and see us again soon.'

It might be an unusual marriage, but Rosa refused to believe that Adrian Pickard harboured any sinister intentions toward his wife. He couldn't have been more relaxed or at ease on the two occasions she had met him. She liked to think that ten years spent practising in the criminal courts had sharpened her natural scepticism and enabled her to detect deviousness in human behaviour. Indeed, she sometimes worried that cynicism was becoming her instant response to her clients' problems. A certain amount was natural, even desirable, in a criminal lawyer, but she had no wish to turn into a total cynic. She knew one or two members of her profession whose cynicism was as unattractive as a facial skin disease.

She had a busy week ahead of her and didn't call the Pickards again until the following weekend. Once more it was Adrian who answered.

'Margaret's in the garden,' he said. 'Shall I get her?'

'Oh, no. Please don't bother her. I only called to see how you both were. Any excitements in the village since we last spoke?'

'The Cuckfields' butler has left. He was part of a married couple. He buttled and his wife cooked, but they walked out on Thursday.'

'Taking the family silver with them?'

'No, it was a straightforward case of incompatibility between Sir Denzil and the man. Things just came to a head. But I understand they have a Portuguese couple taking over shortly. Meanwhile, they're managing with a team of dailies from the village.'

It struck Rosa that Adrian was as well informed as a village postmaster could be on what was going on.

'The only other bit of news,' he went on, 'is that Ivy's cat has had kittens.'

'Ivy?'

'Mrs Ives, one of my assistants.'

'It's all departures and arrivals,' Rosa said. 'Give Margaret my love.'

'I will. I know she'll want me to send you hers.'

The following weekend Peter and Rosa flew to Paris for a couple of nights. It was the sort of extravagance Peter enjoyed organising and over which Rosa's protests grew increasingly feeble. She still had an inherited streak of puritanism in her nature, but it remained muffled for most of the time, thanks to Peter's influence.

It was on the Thursday following their return that Ben greeted Rosa's arrival in the office after a morning in court with, 'Isn't Greenborough the place where your aunt lives, Miss E?'

Ben was Snaith and Epton's young outdoor clerk, who was always willing to turn his hand to anything and was frequently asked to do so. He was particularly adept at spotting newspaper items affecting the firm's clients.

'She isn't actually an aunt,' Rosa said. 'She's my godmother. Why do you ask?'

'There's been a murder there,' Ben replied cheerfully.

Rosa felt her legs go suddenly weak.

'Where'd you read this?' she managed to say.

'In the midday paper. It's only a tiny piece. Says a body has been found in the grounds of some school and foul play is suspected.'

'Were any names mentioned?'

Ben shook his head. 'Said the police hadn't yet identified the body.'

'Was it a man or a woman?' Rosa asked, holding her breath.

'It was a bloke.'

Rosa turned away. She didn't want Ben to see how shaken she was by his news. For one terrible moment she had wondered if Margaret was the victim. She felt compelled to phone the Pickards, but, after speaking to Peter, agreed it would be better to wait until further details were available. As Peter pointed out, the Pickards would very quickly have got in touch with her if they were in any way involved.

'Would you like me to come round this evening?' Peter asked.

'Better not, or I'll never be ready for court in the morning.'

'What's the case?'

'Arson. A young man set fire to his girl-friend's house after she had given him the heave-ho.'

'Anyone hurt?'

'Fortunately not.'

'Any defence?'

'Absolutely none as far as I can see.'

'Well, tell me all about it when we have dinner tomorrow evening. I'll call for you at seven thirty.'

'I'll be ready.'

The next day's papers contained a few more details of Greenborough's suspected foul play, though the body of the man had still not been identified nor the cause of death established.

It was just before seven thirty in the evening when Rosa was expecting Peter to arrive that her telephone rang.

'Rosa?' said an instantly recognisable voice. 'I'm phoning because something very upsetting has happened. There's been a murder – at least, that's the police assumption.'

'I saw something in the paper,' Rosa broke in. 'Is it someone you knew who was killed?'

'No, nothing like that. But the police have been interrogating Adrian. They seem to think he knows something about it. It's too absurd for words.'

'Would you like me to come down this evening?'

'It would be a great kindness.'

'I'll get Peter to drive me. We were about to go out to dinner, but we'll set off for Greenborough instead. Is Adrian home now?'

'No, he's not back yet. He agreed to go to the police station. I'll be so relieved to see you.' She paused before adding, 'It's all a terrible misunderstanding.'

Rosa's heart sank at the sound of these ominous words. She had heard them so often and had come to regard them as a death knell to a client's hopes.

5

Darkness had fallen by the time they reached Greenborough and all the lights in the Pickard's cottage were on. Margaret had obviously been keeping her ears open for she opened the front door before Rosa could ring the bell.

'Is Adrian back?' Rosa enquired as she stepped inside.

'He returned about twenty minutes ago. At least the police brought him back in the car. He'll be down in a few minutes. He's terribly tired and not a little anxious over what's happened. Who wouldn't be in the circumstances?'

'Have the police been able to identify the dead man?'

'It's somebody called Harry Wells. He's not local.'

'Why should the police think that Adrian can help them over his death?'

'It seems this man Wells was in the post office a couple of days ago and began behaving in an offensive manner towards Mrs Ives who was serving. Adrian told him to quieten down and mind his language and the man turned on him. Adrian is quite capable of dealing with rowdies and in no time at all had evicted him. The man cursed and swore and started hurling threats around. He said he'd make Adrian regret his attitude.'

There was the sound of someone coming downstairs and a moment later Adrian appeared. He came across and kissed Rosa on the cheek and then shook hands with Peter.

'Margaret shouldn't have troubled you,' he said with a wan smile. 'It's not as if I'm under arrest, or anything as dramatic as that. I don't know how much Margaret has told you.'

'Just that this man Wells made a nuisance of himself in the post office, that you evicted him and he departed uttering threats,' Margaret said.

Adrian nodded slowly. 'That was two days ago and yesterday his dead body was found.'

'What did he die of?' Rosa asked.

'I understand drowning was the actual cause of death, but that he was probably already unconscious at the time. It seems he had been knocked out by a heavy blow to the head and then been held face down in a stream.'

Rosa frowned. 'Was this in the grounds of the school?'

'Yes, Warren Hall School. There's a copse on the far side of the playing fields which has a stagnant stream passing through it. The body was found there early yesterday morning.'

'Who by?'

'Joe Atherly. His cottage is on the farther side of the copse.'

'Presumably he's also been thoroughly questioned by the police?'

'Presumably.'

A silence fell, broken when Rosa said, 'What I don't understand, Adrian, is why the police have trained their sights on you. The fact that you threw this man out of the post office might give him a motive to get back at you, but not the other way about.'

Adrian stared vacantly across the room, but made no reply.

'You'd better tell Rosa the whole story,' Margaret said.

Adrian gave a reluctant nod. 'I usually go for a walk before retiring for the night,' he began. 'I've not been used to going to bed before the small hours and I find it difficult to get to sleep without filling my lungs with fresh air. It's all that living on ships. It so happens that on the evening Harry Wells met his death, I went for a walk in the grounds of Warren Hall School.'

'What time was that?' Rosa broke in.

'Between eleven thirty and midnight.'

'And I suppose somebody saw you?'

Adrian nodded. 'Yes, Bruce Thurston.'

'What was he doing out at that hour?'

'He was on his way home after dining with the Cuckfields. It's the school holidays, but he's not gone away yet.'

'Did you speak to him?'

'We had a brief word after I'd identified myself. In a sense I was trespassing and he shouted at me to find out what I was doing.'

'Did he behave perfectly reasonably once he knew who you were?'

'Yes, though he must have told the police he'd met me.'

'That doesn't strike me as unreasonable,' Rosa remarked. 'What line have the police been taking with you?'

'They're suggesting that I bumped into Wells while I was out walking, that he attacked me and in the course of defending myself, I knocked him out and then pushed him face down into the stream.'

'In other words, they're inviting you to confess to manslaughter.'

'Yes. They kept saying they didn't believe I'd deliberately murdered him, though lawyers might take a different view if they thought I'd held his head under water.'

'The carrot and stick approach,' Rosa observed. She gave Adrian a quizzical look. 'Can I take it you've not made any admissions?'

'I told them what I've told you, which is the truth.'

'What do you know about Harry Wells? Where does he come from and what brought him to Greenborough? Presumably it wasn't simply to buy stamps at the post office?'

'I gathered from one of the officers I spoke to that he comes from Woolwich. One of his brothers arrived at the station to identify his body while I was there. He lived with a widowed mother. As to what he was doing in Greenborough, I don't think anyone has found out.'

'What sort of age was he?'

'Somewhere in his forties I heard an officer say.'

'What was the nature of the trouble he caused in the post office?'

'He'd obviously been drinking and became stroppy when he found he had to join a queue to be served. He became abusive and shouted at Mrs Ives. Fortunately, I was there and could intervene. I don't think anyone could blame me for throwing him out.'

'Of course they couldn't,' Margaret said robustly. Turning to Rosa she went on, 'What do you think Adrian ought to do now?'

'That depends on the next police move. Did they say they'd want to interview you further?'

Adrian bit his lip. 'I certainly got that impression.'

'The important thing is not to make any admissions. You can always demand the presence of a lawyer and I'll certainly come and hold your hand if you wish . . .'

'I'd be very grateful if you would, Rosa.'

'I'd been going to add that if you have a solicitor, you ought to get in touch with him.'

'I'd far sooner you acted for me.'

'All right. You have my office and home telephone numbers, so feel free to call at any time. By the way, do you know the name of the officer in charge of the investigation?'

'Detective Chief Inspector Stanwick.'

'I realise you'll be wanting to get back to London, Rosa dear,' Margaret now said. 'What can I offer you before you leave?'

'I'd love a milky decaffeinated coffee.'

'Everyone to his own taste. What about you, Peter?'

'Coffee for me, too, please, but black. And preferably not decaffeinated.'

'I'm afraid we've ruined your evening,' Margaret went on after Adrian had departed to the kitchen, 'but you have our combined gratitude.' She paused. 'I still don't entirely understand why the police have picked on Adrian.'

Nor for that matter did Rosa.

It was close on midnight when she and Peter left to drive home.

'How did Adrian's story sound to you?' Rosa asked as the car pulled away from the Pickard's cottage.

'As thin as the paper of a Chinese lantern,' Peter replied.

'You didn't believe him?'

'Did you?'

'It seemed plausible,' Rosa said with a touch of hesitation. 'At what point do you think he was lying?'

'I don't say he actually lied, but I felt he was out to create a certain impression, which wasn't, I suspect, an entirely honest one.'

'Explain.'

'The whole business of these late night walks struck me as odd.'

'A lot of people do take walks before going to bed.'

'I know, but I have a feeling Adrian went out for more than a lungful of night air.'

'Such as?'

'I've no idea.'

'You don't actually believe he may have been responsible for Wells' death?'

'I certainly don't want to believe it, but it's a strange story. And I hope for your godmother's sake it'll have a happy ending.'

6

Detective Chief Inspector Neil Stanwick was a modern police officer with some old-fashioned ideas. He had been born in the county and had grown up in a village not far from Greenborough. He had done well at school and had completed his education at London University where he had taken a degree in law. He was happily married with a son aged eight and a daughter two years younger. Nobody doubted that he would end up as a chief constable. He had reached his present rank at the age of thirty-three. He was stationed at Havenbridge, a market town about a dozen miles east of Greenborough, and was the senior CID officer in the district.

He was now sitting in a small office at Greenborough police station which smelt strongly of lavender furniture polish. He supposed there were worse smells to endure and tried to feel grateful that someone had taken the trouble to greet him with a clean office. Like many village police stations, Greenborough's no longer functioned on a full-time basis, being open only for a few hours three days a week. It was a state of affairs Stanwick deplored. In his view the only way to defeat crime was to have policemen visible on every street corner. That would be far more effective than relying on a lot of gadgetry. As for all the paperwork required of the police, it had turned them all into pen-pushing clerks. It wasn't that he had anything against modern technology. He hadn't, but held that it should assist a policeman, not displace him.

On the desk in front of him lay an array of objects found on the dead man's body. One item in particular interested him; in fact the only one. It was an old brown envelope with a cellophane window that had originally emanated from the gas board. It was empty, but had a name scribbled on the back.

'Now, why,' he asked himself, 'should Harry Wells have been carrying a piece of paper bearing Lady Cuckfield's name?'

Wells' brother, who had identified the body, had been unable to help. He had told the police he had no idea what had brought Harry to Greenborough. He didn't see Harry very often and though he visited his mother from time to time, his brother was usually out.

'Presumably you knew he had a police record?' Stanwick had said.

The older Wells had nodded. 'He's been inside once or twice. Me and my other brother didn't much like the idea of him living with our mum, but he was the youngest and she'd always had a soft spot for him.' He had shrugged. 'And to give Harry his due, he was fond of her, too. She'd probably have had to move into a home if Harry hadn't been there to do things for her. So . . . well, it seemed like a good arrangement.'

'Was Harry ever married?' Stanwick had asked.

'Married and divorced. He and Liz split up years ago.'

'Any children?'

'No.'

And that had been the end of that interview. Stanwick now got up from the desk and stretched. Most investigations offered a choice of starting-points and a visit to Greenborough Court seemed the obvious one in this case. He sat down again and reached for the telephone.

'I'd like to speak to Lady Cuckfield,' he said when a foreign voice answered.

'I see,' the voice replied doubtfully.

52

'Is Lady Cuckfield at home?' Stanwick asked.

'Wait, I see.' The receiver was put down with a clatter. When it was picked up again a different voice said, 'Lady Cuckfield speaking, who is that?'

'Detective Chief Inspector Stanwick, Lady Cuckfield. Would it be convenient if I came and saw you?'

'I'm afraid my husband's not here. He's in London for the day.'

'It's you I wish to speak to.'

'Oh . . . oh . . . can you tell me what it's about?'

'Certainly. I'm investigating the death of one Harry Wells whose body was found in the grounds of Warren Hall School.'

'Oh, yes, of course I've heard about it. But I'm afraid there's nothing I know which would help you, Chief Inspector.'

'Nevertheless, I'd still like to see you.'

'Well, all right. I'll be in for the rest of the morning.'

'I'll come straightaway.'

'Will it take long, whatever it is?'

'I'll take up as little of your time as possible,' Stanwick said courteously.

WPC Blake was in the station and he decided to take her with him. The employment of female police officers was something of which he thoroughly approved.

'I gather Sir Denzil Cuckfield is a proper country gent,' WPC Blake observed when they were on their way.

'What you really mean,' Stanwick said with a smile, 'is that he's a crusty old bastard. Anyway, he won't be there, he's in London. And it's Lady Cuckfield I want to see, not Sir Denzil, so I'm quite glad he's out of the way. He can be rather intimidating, I believe.'

A manservant opened the door when they arrived and invited them in by a series of hand signals. Stanwick assumed he was the person who had originally answered the phone.

They were led across a wide hall to a door on the left. The man knocked on it and then flung it open. Lady Cuckfield was standing in the middle of the room in a pose of seeming indecision.

'It would really have been better if you had waited until my husband was back,' she said as she shook hands with them. 'If anyone can help you, it'll be he, though I don't think he knows anything that isn't common knowledge. Have you been able to find out what the dead man was doing in Greenborough?'

'That's where you may be able to help, Lady Cuckfield.' He reached into his pocket and pulled out the envelope on which her name was written. 'This was found in the deceased's possession.' It was now in its own cellophane wrapping and he handed it to her.

'But why's it got my name on it?' she asked in a startled voice.

'Do you recognise the writing?'

'No.'

'Can you think of any reason why the dead man should have had a piece of paper bearing your name?'

'None whatsoever. It's a total mystery.'

'Wells must have got your name from somewhere.'

'I'm afraid I can't help you over that. We've had a number of staff changes in the past twelve months. Maybe he was given our name by an ex-employee and came here looking for work.'

'That's a possibility,' Stanwick said and went on, 'Have you received any out-of-the-way letters or phone calls recently?'

'We get the occasional phone call from some crank who tells us our heads will roll when the revolution comes.' She sighed. 'But whoever he is, I'm sure he's harmless.'

Stanwick looked at her thoughtfully. Lady Cuckfield struck him as an essentially simple woman without any pretensions. He reckoned she was about sixty, perhaps a little less. She was dressed without affectation and her hair, which was grey, was brushed back from her forehead.

'I'm afraid you've had rather a wasted journey, Chief Inspector,' she said, breaking the silence that had fallen. 'But I did tell you I knew nothing which was likely to assist your investigation.' She glanced towards the door. 'If there's nothing else . . .'

'What did you make of her?' Stanwick asked WPC Blake as they drove away from the house.

'She was more nervous at the beginning than when we left.'

'That was my impression, too. I wonder why? Obviously I didn't manage to exploit the cause of her nervousness. My guess would be that I'm ignorant of something she'd sooner I didn't know about. Once she realised that she ceased to be nervous.'

'Most people have things they'd prefer the police not to know about,' WPC Blake said. 'I know I have.'

'You're right. There's a skeleton in almost every family cupboard. The question is whether Lady Cuckfield's is relevant to my investigation.'

7

Bruce Thurston had been headmaster of Warren Hall School for three years, having taken it over from his father who had suffered a crippling heart attack in 1987. Bruce was the third generation of Thurstons to be running the school. Though married, he and his wife had no children, so there was no question of it being handed on to a fourth generation.

They had not been an easy three years, but somehow the school had kept going. The economics of maintaining a private boarding school became more difficult with every year that passed. Fees were regularly increased, though there was a limit to the amount parents would (or could) pay to have their sons privately educated. Already a number who had registered their boys' names for future entry had cancelled for financial reasons.

Though it had been established for the best part of a century, Warren Hall had never achieved the highest status. Its academic record was unspectacular, though from time to time one of its pupils would win a scholarship to one of the minor public schools.

The discovery of a dead body on school property was something Bruce Thurston could have done without. At least it had happened during the holidays. If the boys had been in residence, it would all have been a hundred times worse. The disappearance of Stephen Willett in 1932 still haunted the school. Bruce's grandfather who had been headmaster at the time was said never to have fully recovered from the event and its dramatic aftermath.

A few years after that, his grandfather had struggled to keep the school going during the war and had, with considerable relief, handed the headmastership over to his own son (Bruce's father) as soon as he came out of the navy in 1946.

Thurston rose from his desk and went over to the window from where he could observe Joe Atherly's approach. Now seventy-six, Joe was a good deal fitter than many men who had not yet reached their three score years and ten. He had phoned Joe that morning and asked him if he could spare half an hour. If Joe had wondered what about, he never asked. He watched Joe enter the building and waited for a knock on his study door.

'Come in,' he called out, when it came. 'Thank you for coming, Joe. Sit down and make yourself comfortable. How's Mrs Atherly?'

'Poorly.'

'I'm sorry to hear that. If I'm right she's known the school even longer than you have.'

Joe nodded. 'Her father was groundsman during the twenties and thirties.'

Joe waited with a watchful air. He knew he had not been asked over to reminisce about old times. He had a shrewd idea what was on the headmaster's mind, but it was up to Thurston to state his business.

'This fellow Wells, whose body you found, what do you know about him?'

'Never seen him before in my life.'

'Any idea what he was doing in Greenborough?'

'Total stranger as far as I'm concerned,' Joe said.

'Have the police found out anything about him?'

'Not likely to tell me if they have.'

'I suppose they've asked you if you knew him?'

'And I told them I didn't, just as I'm telling you.'

'Have there ever been any Wells's in the village?'

'Not as I know of.' He paused. 'Though I believe there was a local girl who married a chap of that name, but it was a long time back. And she'd gone away from Greenborough before she got married.'

'What was her name?'

'Don't recall,' Joe replied, staring out of the window at a thrush on the lawn.

'Are you sure you don't recall her name?'

'I've told you I don't. Anyway, why are you so interested?'

The headmaster looked taken aback by the tone of Joe's voice.

'I think I have a right to be interested. After all, the body was found on my property.' Fixing Joe with a hard stare, he went on, 'You must remember the time that boy disappeared in the thirties. What do you think happened to him?'

'To young Willett?'

'You must have given it a lot of thought.'

Joe shrugged. 'He's probably dead by now, anyway.'

'You mean you don't believe he was murdered?'

'He may have been.'

'Why do you say he's probably dead anyway?'

'Killed in the war likely as not.'

'Which do you think the more likely?'

Joe was silent for a while, then said, 'Best leave the past alone. If Wally Price killed the boy, he'll be being tormented in hell. If he didn't, someone else will be.'

Bruce Thurston doubted whether Joe had ever heard of the Delphic oracle, but thought she might have been proud of such a cryptic pronouncement.

Shortly after this Joe took his leave and walked home.

'What did he want?' his wife enquired when he arrived back.

'He thinks there's some connection between Harry Wells' death and what happened when Willett disappeared back in the thirties.'

'Did he say that?'

'No, but he believes it. It's plain that he's worried about the effect it could have on the school, particularly if the newspapers resurrect the earlier business.'

'Which, given half a chance, they'll do.'

Gwen Atherly rose stiffly from the chair on which she had been sitting. Every movement was a painful effort, with some days worse than others.

'What was the name of that girl who went off and later married a man named Wells?'

'You mean the one . . .'

'Yes, that one.'

'Why?'

'Just tell me what her name was.'

'Norma Kirk. Wouldn't have thought you'd have forgotten it.'

'Can't remember names these days.'

His wife gave him a thoughtful look. 'Are you keeping something back? Something you're not telling the police . . . or me?'

'The arthritis has got into your brain, woman,' he said sharply, turning away.

8

'Mr Pickard phoned and would like you to call him back,' Stephanie said when Rosa returned to the office the following day after a morning in court. 'He's at this number,' she added, handing Rosa a slip of paper.

Rosa glanced at it and frowned. It wasn't the telephone number of the cottage and she assumed it must be a line to the post office itself.

As she walked along to her room, she wondered what could have happened since she and Peter had driven down the previous evening. She was still troubled by their visit, in particular by Peter's distinctly downbeat reaction. She respected his instinct and judgement as much as she relied on her own.

Sitting down at her desk she tapped out the dialling code and the number Stephanie had written down. It was some while before anyone answered and then it was a female voice.

'Is Mr Pickard there?' Rosa asked.

'Hold on, he's just coming,'

A groundswell of background noise was suddenly blotted out as a door closed and she heard Adrian's voice.

'Is that Rosa?' he asked.

'Yes, where are you speaking from?'

'It's a call box inside the post office. I've closed the door, so we can't be overheard. I'm coming up to London tomorrow and would like to see you. On business, I mean. May I come along to the office?'

'I'll be here in the afternoon. What time?'

'Early rather than late.'

'Two thirty?'

'That'll be fine. Incidentally, Margaret knows I'm coming up to town, but I've not told her I propose to visit you, so I'd be grateful if you didn't mention it to her.' He went on quickly, 'Don't worry, I promise not to embarrass you.'

Rosa put down the receiver wishing she could feel sure of this. There was something ominous in his not wanting his wife to know of his proposed visit to her office.

He arrived on the dot of two thirty the next afternoon and was escorted to her office by Ben, who lingered long enough to see him kiss Rosa on the cheek and report the event to Stephanie.

'It's ages since I was last in this part of London,' he said, as he sat down in her visitor's chair.

'It's not exactly a fashionable area,' Rosa remarked. 'But then Snaith and Epton doesn't have a fashionable clientele.'

'Mostly here today and gone tomorrow types, I imagine?'

'That's one way of describing them.' She gave Adrian a pointed look. 'Is Margaret still unaware of your visit?'

'Yes, I told her I was going to see my accountant. I was due to pay him a visit, anyway.' He shifted uncomfortably in his chair. 'I'm afraid I didn't tell you the entire truth the other evening. I'm a bit more involved in events than I made out. The fact is that I spotted Wells when I was out walking that night and I followed him. After what had happened in the post office, I was curious to find out what he was up to.'

'How did you recognise him in the dark?'

'There was a full moon that dived in and out of cloud and at times one could see everything.'

'Did he see you?'

'I don't think so. He was too intent on his own business. I'm pretty sure he was on his way to meet someone. When he entered the copse on the far side of the playing fields, I lost sight of him. I could hear him moving about and then there was a confusion of sounds, followed by total silence. I decided to retrace my steps and shortly afterwards Mr Thurston shouted at me.'

'Could he have been in the copse?'

'I suppose so, though it didn't occur to me at the time. Quite frankly, I was embarrassed at being discovered on his property at that hour of the night.'

'Did you see Wells again?'

'No.'

'Or anyone else?'

'No.'

'And it was Mr Thurston who put the police on to you?'

'Yes.'

'It may have been a shrewd move on his part. Get your own blow in first.'

'You don't seriously think Thurston killed this fellow?'

'Somebody killed him and Thurston had the opportunity.'

'But what possible motive could he have had?'

'That's quite a different matter. Until we know what Harry Wells was doing in Greenborough, motive remains a mystery.'

'You can see why I've not told Margaret what I've just told you. The last thing I want is to worry her unnecessarily.'

What Rosa would like to have known was whether he had now told her the whole truth, but she decided to let her client continue unprompted.

Adrian went on, 'We don't have to inform the police, do we? I don't want to become any further involved in their investigation.'

'We had best play that by ear. There's certainly no reason to dash off immediately and add to what you've already told them. On the other hand if they find out that you've been withholding information it won't look so good. They'll jump to the conclusion that you have something to hide. Something which would prove your involvement in Wells' death.'

'But that's awful!' Adrian exclaimed.

'Bearing in mind that the police have already put pressure on you to confess to the killing, they'd soon exert even more.'

'I feel as if I'm being set up,' Adrian said miserably.

'Who by?'

'By someone who's out to save his own skin.'

'Nothing unusual about that. It's *sauve qui peut* when there are several suspects in the ring.'

'But I seem to be the only one.'

'There's also Joe Atherly who found the body and Bruce Thurston who was out and about that night. I'm sure the police will be searching hard for a motive. Primarily a motive for Harry Wells coming to Greenborough. Once that has been established, a lot of other pieces will fall into place.'

A few minutes later Adrian Pickard rose.

'Thank you for seeing me, Rosa. I feel better now that I've told you the whole truth.'

'If I've not been very helpful, it's because it's difficult to offer advice in a situation like this.'

'I didn't expect you to wave a magic wand.' He walked to the door and paused. 'I'll keep you in touch with developments. With luck the police'll lose interest in me.'

But will they? Rosa wondered after he had gone. She could see a rough time ahead for her client. He was far from out of the wood.

She got up from her desk and went along to her partner's room.

'You look bothered,' Robin said cheerfully, as she flopped into a chair.

'I am.'

'You're beginning to wish that your oft-married godmother hadn't come back into your life?' Observing Rosa's expression, he went on, 'Stephanie told me who your visitor was. So what did the ship's pianist want?'

'He obviously felt that a trouble shared was a trouble halved.'

'I've always thought that a pretty silly saying. It depends entirely with whom you share the trouble. Pick the wrong person and you can double it. Anyway, tell me what's happened.'

When she finished her recital of events, Robin let out a sigh. 'Your problem is that you know so little about Pickard. And the same goes for your gallivanting godmother. I know you're fond of her and want to believe that everything is fine and dandy, but hasn't the time come to take off your rose-tinted spectacles?'

'What exactly do you mean, Robin?'

'What I mean is that for all you know about him, Adrian Pickard could be a mass murderer.'

9

Norma Wells lived in a terraced house in one of the older parts of Woolwich. She had been there for over fifty years, first as a married woman and for the past thirty years as a widow. The address was 28 Volga Close, SE18.

When her husband died suddenly in 1960, Brian, her eldest son, was twenty-one and Toby, her next, was nineteen. Both of them were earning, which meant that only Harry, who had been born in 1946, was dependent on her. She had often reflected that fourteen was probably the worst possible age for a boy to lose his father. She was sure it accounted for Harry's troubled adolescence, the scrapes he had got into and the worry he had caused her. But he was still her son, her youngest, and he had always had a special place in her affections.

When Detective Chief Inspector Stanwick, accompanied by WPC Blake, called to visit her, he was soon aware of the strong ties between mother and son. She received them in the small front room, which was obviously put to infrequent use. The atmosphere was stale, but inoffensively so.

She looked frail and gave the appearance of still being in a state of shock. She moved slowly and held on to items of furniture as she did so.

'I suffer from angina,' she said, in what could have been taken as a tone of reproach.

'I know what a misery that can be,' Stanwick said sympathetically. 'My father-in-law suffers from it as well.'

'I don't know how I'm going to manage with Harry gone. I don't want to end up in one of those homes for old people.'

Stanwick clucked in sympathy and after a short interval felt he could properly broach the matter that had brought him to her home.

'Did Harry tell you he was going to Greenborough?'

She shook her head. 'He just said he'd probably be away for the night. When that happened he used to tell Mrs Archer next door so that she'd know I was on my own and would keep an eye on me. I have very good neighbours, but it's not the same as having Harry here.'

'Did he give you any idea at all where he was going?'

'No, he was always going to different places.'

'Doing what?'

'Buying things to sell in the market.'

'Was that his main business?'

'Yes, he'd go to sales at big houses and come back with bibs and bobs which he'd sell down at the market.'

Stanwick knew the pattern well. He doubted whether many of Harry's bibs and bobs were honestly acquired. It looked as if his visit to Greenborough had been a burglarious outing, with the Cuckfields' house his prime target. An approach via the school grounds and the copse in which his body was found also fitted that scenario. What didn't fit was his disruptive presence in the post office earlier in the day. That had been like leaving a calling card, something more intelligent burglars refrained from doing.

'Had Harry ever mentioned Greenborough to you, Mrs Wells?'

She appeared to flinch slightly, but slowly shook her head.

'I feel an attack coming on,' she said, putting a hand up to her heart. 'I must take a tablet.' She glanced at WPC Blake. 'They're on the kitchen table.'

WPC Blake sprang up and hurried from the room to return a few seconds later with a bottle of tablets and a glass of water. Mrs Wells waved aside the water and popped a tablet under her tongue.

They watched her as she sat back with her eyes closed.

'We can't leave her like this, sir,' WPC Blake said in a worried voice.

Stanwick took one of Mrs Wells' hands and held it in his. 'I'm sorry if our visit has distressed you, but we'll leave now and not bother you any further. Would you like me to tell your neighbour that you've had a bad turn?'

'Mrs Archer'll know what to do,' she said weakly.

Mrs Archer, who proved to be a brisk, no-nonsense sort of woman, was considerably younger than Mrs Wells.

'She oughtn't to be there on her own,' she declared. 'I've told Brian – that's her eldest son – but he said his mother didn't want to move. Maybe she doesn't, but she needs looking after and I can't be popping in and out all day. And then there's nights. Trouble is she's never got on with Brian's wife.'

'What about her other son?'

'Works on a North Sea oil rig. Has a wife in Hertfordshire and a mistress in Aberdeen. He sends his mother money from time to time, but that's about their only contact. Anyway, I'll see how she is a bit later on, and if I think it's necessary I'll call her doctor.' She looked Stanwick up and down. 'So you're investigating Harry's death?'

Stanwick nodded. 'Do you know anything that might help me?'

'Norma – that's Mrs Wells – has spent her life making excuses for Harry, but if you want my opinion, he was just a bad lot. I'm not surprised he came to a sticky end.'

'Do you have any idea what he was doing in Greenborough?'

'None. I'd never even heard of the place.'

'How often does Mrs Wells have these attacks?'

'Stress brings them on. And she's got enough of that at the moment with Harry's death.' She shot Stanwick a sharp look. 'And visits from the police don't help to relax a person.'

As they threaded their way through London's south-eastern suburbs and headed for home, Stanwick felt his investigation was moving in the right direction. He now thought it likely that Harry Wells had disturbed someone, who like himself was up to no good, and had been killed for his pains. The person concerned had initially knocked him out and had then obviously decided it was too risky to leave him alive.

There were two people he must interview again as a follow-up to this theory. Joe Atherly and Adrian Pickard. Stanwick was sure that Atherly could tell him more, if so minded. Even though an old man, he was physically fit and knew the copse and surrounding area better than anyone. Everyone knew he did a bit of poaching. Equally well known was Sir Denzil Cuckfield's implacable attitude towards poachers. Moreover he was a local magistrate and wielded considerable clout in the neighbourhood. If Wells had surprised Joe setting snares, the threat of exposure could have caused Joe to lash out in panic.

As for Adrian Pickard, Stanwick had still to make up his mind. People who took midnight walks aroused his suspicion and when they left dead bodies in their wake . . . Stanwick still considered it a tenable theory that Pickard had bumped into Wells in the course of his nocturnal perambulation, that a fight had developed and that he had used more force than the law would consider necessary to fend off Wells' assault.

Admittedly Pickard had stoutly denied this, but it still remained a plausible theory.

By all accounts Wells was a fairly worthless member of society whose death would be mourned by nobody other than his mother. But even society's more worthless members were entitled not to be held face down in stagnant water and, when this did happen, to have their deaths as fully investigated as those of worthier citizens. As far as Stanwick was concerned, Harry Wells' killer would be pursued without respite until the enquiry was brought to a successful conclusion. Atherly and Pickard had emerged as prime suspects. Eliminate one and the other would become as oven-ready as a Christmas turkey. That, at least, was how he saw things as he returned to Greenborough that afternoon.

10

'I'm surprised Martin hasn't been in touch,' Sir Denzil remarked as he sipped a pink gin before lunch the next day.

'He phoned this morning,' his wife said.

'Oh? What did he have to say?'

'He's very busy. Even though parliament is in recess, he goes to the ministry every day.'

'I suppose the minister's gone on holiday and left Martin holding the fort. Did he say whether he was coming down?'

'He said he thought it would be better to wait until the trouble has blown over.'

'What trouble?' Sir Denzil asked sharply.

'The death of this man Wells.'

'Can't see why that should keep Martin away.'

'He's got his public image to think about.'

Sir Denzil snorted. 'Some ne'er-do-well being found dead in the grounds of Warren Hall can't affect Martin's reputation as a junior minister.'

'You know what the tabloid press is like. They'd spread it all over their front pages if they thought it'd sell a few additional copies.' She paused. 'Anyway, I agreed it was better he should stay away until the dust has settled.'

'I've never heard such nonsense in all my life. The press has never taken any interest in Martin's visits here before. It might be as well if I had a word with Chief Inspector Stanwick myself. I'll find out how his enquiry is going. Then I'll speak to Martin and tell him he has nothing to worry about. In any event, I want to discuss various estate matters with him.'

'Why don't you have lunch with him in London?'

'Because I have a full list of appointments on the days I go up and if I have lunch at all, it's a boardroom snack.'

He usually went up to London twice a week, returning home by four o'clock. His wife had the impression that boardroom snacks were often served in glasses.

Lunch at Greenborough Court, on the other hand, was a frugal meal, unless there happened to be guests, and the main meal of the day was served in the evening.

'This is an excellent bit of Stilton,' Sir Denzil remarked as he balanced a lump on a piece of crispbread and conveyed it precariously to his mouth. 'You don't know what you're missing,' he added as he watched his wife peeling a grape.

'I've never cared for strong cheeses,' she said.

You've never cared for strong anything, he felt like saying, but didn't.

He swallowed what was in his mouth and pushed back his chair. Without a further word he walked from the room and she heard him go into his study and close the door.

She was used to his churlish ways and ignored them. He was eleven years older than she and they had met at a dance in Derbyshire where she had grown up. Martin had been a honeymoon baby, but thereafter she had been unable to bear further children, which had been a sadness to her and a frustration to her husband who had felt it reflected on his virility. They had moved into Greenborough Court a few years after their wedding when his parents had died in a hotel fire in the South of France. Though she was of a diffident disposition which many people took for weakness, she had a strong, stubborn streak to fortify her at times of crisis.

In his study, Sir Denzil picked up the telephone and tapped out a number.

'I wish to speak to Detective Chief Inspector Stanwick,' he said when the connection was made. 'Tell him it's Sir Denzil Cuckfield on the line.' He let out a mild belch, the result of a second helping of Stilton cheese.

'Good afternoon, Sir Denzil,' Stanwick said a few moments later. 'What can I do for you?'

'What you can do is tell me how your enquiries are progressing,' Sir Denzil replied, nettled by Stanwick's apparently off-hand tone.

'Satisfactorily, I'm pleased to say.'

'Are you close to making an arrest?'

'I hope so.'

'May I enquire on whom you have your sights trained?'

'I'm afraid I'm not at liberty to discuss details, sir.'

'If you ask me, there's something fishy about this new postmaster chap. I gather you've had him in for interview?'

'That's so.'

'Think he may have done it?'

'Mr Pickard's been helping us with our enquiries, along with various other people.'

'Including my wife,' Sir Denzil said aggressively.

'Lady Cuckfield was most helpful,' Stanwick replied in the same unruffled tone.

'Well, I hope you'll clear the matter up quickly. Meanwhile, if there's anything I can do, let me know.'

'Thank you, Sir Denzil,' Stanwick replied with a faint touch of irony.

As soon as their conversation was concluded, Sir Denzil put through a call to his son.

'I hear you spoke to your mother this morning,' he said.

'Yes, she told me you were out.'

'Never mind that. I gather you agreed between you that it would be better if you didn't come down to Greenborough until things have been cleared up. By which I mean the death of this fellow Wells. Personally I see no reason whatsoever for you to stay away.'

'It so happens, father, that I'm particularly busy at the moment. The ministry's responsible for a major bill in the next session of parliament and I don't have any time for excursions out of London during the coming week or two. Even my constituency won't see much of me.'

'Nevertheless, I want you to come down. I have a number of family matters I wish to discuss. You could drive down for dinner one evening and back to town again afterwards. Which day'll suit you?'

'I'll have to consult my diary. It'll be best if I call you back.'

His tone conveyed a degree of resentment.

'Good. Incidentally, I was talking to Chief Inspector Stanwick just before I called you. I told him I thought he ought to look into Pickard's background. There's something distinctly odd about the fellow. And as for that painted old crone he has for a wife . . . well, he's young enough to be her son, almost her grandson. They've only been married a short time. Met on a cruise apparently. He's clearly a fortune hunter and she, from all accounts, has the fortune.'

'What did Stanwick have to say?'

'He wasn't giving anything away.'

'I must ring off, father. I have a meeting about to start.'

'All right, but mind you call me back. And Martin?'

'Yes, father?'

'Discuss these sort of things with me rather than your mother.'

Martin Cuckfield put the telephone down and stared across his pleasant room. Ministers of State were well looked after when it came to office furnishings. Martin's ambitions, however, were pitched still higher. He hoped eventually to have a seat in the cabinet, which meant his luck would have to hold for quite some time yet.

Sir Denzil, meanwhile, decided to make one further call.

'That you, Thurston?' he said when a male voice answered.

'Thurston speaking.'

'It's Cuckfield here. Tell me, what do you make of this fellow Pickard at the post office?'

'What makes you ask?' the headmaster of Warren Hall enquired in a wary tone.

'I'm sure he's up to something. What was he doing when you caught him on your property the night you dined with us?'

'He said he was out for a breath of fresh air.'

'Highly suspicious if you ask me. I reckon he could have killed this man Wells.'

'I reported his presence to the police, so it's up to them.'

'Let's hope they take him apart.'

'Personally, I hope the murderer isn't a local person. If the seeds of the crime are planted here, it could affect all our lives.'

'That sounds a bit melodramatic.'

'All I know is that my school still carries the scars of what happened in 1932 and that was twenty years before I was even born.'

'I know. I was at Warren Hall at the time. Did I ever tell you I once slept in the next bed to Willett, the boy who disappeared?'

'Yes.'

'A bit of a loner, as I recall. Dreadful for his parents never knowing what happened to him.'

'I believe it shattered them. I understand they both died soon after the war, having stayed on in India.'

'Of course, I'm not the only person with memories of those days.'

'No, there's Joe Atherly.'

'Joe was a callow youth at the time. Some people thought he dropped Price in the mire to save his own skin. But he's served your school well.'

Bruce Thurston smiled grimly. Faithful old retainer or devious rogue? He knew into which category he would slot Joe Atherly.

11

It had been Robin Snaith's idea that the firm should undergo its own technological revolution. The departure of his personal secretary after twenty years had brought about his change of attitude. She was replaced by a multi-user word processor and a fax machine. Shortly afterwards a computer was installed to take charge of the firm's accounts which had previously been dealt with by old Mr Radford on a part-time basis. It seemed to Rosa that every corner of the office was filled by a piece of machinery ready to break into a purposeful hum at the press of a button.

The supporting staff now consisted of Stephanie, Ben and a typing pool comprising one girl.

'Cutting overheads is the name of the game,' had been Robin's slogan and this had certainly been achieved.

Rosa's word processor sat on a table in a corner of her office and sulked. She had mastered its demonology without too much difficulty, but knew that it could never become a friend in the way her portable Olivetti had. Every time she tapped its keys and watched words swarm over its small green screen, she felt she was observing marine life in an aquarium.

And when it came to interviewing a client she still preferred to make hand-written notes and later translate these into a statement, rather than put words direct into the processor. There was something coldly aloof and impersonal about this concoction of electric impulses and microchips that she found uncongenial.

It was an afternoon two days after Adrian Pickard's visit and Rosa was sitting at her desk out-staring the word processor when her phone rang. She was still brooding over what Robin had said about Adrian, uncomfortably aware that there was nothing she could immediately do to resolve the doubts he had sowed in her mind.

She reached for the receiver.

'Mrs Pickard would like to speak to you,' Stephanie announced. 'Shall I put her through?'

A telephone call from Margaret could only mean a crisis had arisen.

'Is that you, Rosa?' she said huskily.

'Yes, it is, what's happened?'

'Adrian's back at the police station. Can you possibly come down?'

'When you say *back* at the police station—'

'They sent a car for him.'

'He's not under arrest?'

'I've no idea. All I know is that he dashed in about half an hour ago to say they wanted to question him again. He was driven off in broad daylight,' Margaret added indignantly. 'I feel it's most important he has a lawyer at his side.'

'Yes, I'll come,' Rosa said. 'Which police station is he at?'

70

'How would I know? They just drove him away.'

'It may be Havenbridge. That's the divisional headquarters.'

'I'm sure you'll be able to find out.'

Rosa put down the telephone and sighed. Adrian Pickard was taking up more of her time than she had either envisaged or, indeed, wanted. She presumed he had still not told his wife of his visit to Snaith and Epton's office and Rosa could see further difficulties ahead.

Ten minutes later she had ascertained that Adrian was at Havenbridge. She was unable to speak to Chief Inspector Stanwick, but left a message to say she was on her way and that he should not, in the meantime, take any liberties with her client – or words to that effect.

She then phoned Peter and informed his answering machine where she had gone.

It was with a mixture of reluctance and apprehension that she got into her car and set off along all too familiar roads.

She had once done a case in Havenbridge and knew where the police station was. Lights were shining from all its windows when she drew up outside. She locked her car and hurried in. Despite the lights, the station appeared to be deserted. At one end of a counter was a bell push. 'Ring for attention' said a printed notice beside it.

Rosa rang and a grizzled head immediately popped up from below the level of the counter. The head was followed by a body in uniform wearing a sergeant's stripes.

'Hello,' he said amiably. 'I didn't hear you come in. Not been waiting long, have you?' He seemed to regard Rosa's arrival as a welcome relief from what he'd been doing. 'You'll hardly believe this,' he went on, 'but we've got a mouse under here. Artful little bugger, too. We've done everything to catch him, but he's always one move ahead.'

'How do you know it's a he?' Rosa asked, distracted by the thought of a mouse occupying the attention of a large, middle-aged sergeant.

'You're right, it could be a girl mouse.'

'You'd better borrow a cat.'

'One of our policewomen brought in her mother's cat, but it couldn't have shown less interest.' He sighed. 'Anyway, what can I do for you?'

'I understand a client of mine is being interviewed here. I'd like to see him.'

'Is that to do with the killing at Greenborough?'

'Yes.'

'And your name, miss?'

'Rosa Epton. I'm Mr Pickard's solicitor.'

'If you just take a seat, I'll find out what's happening. I only came on duty half an hour ago, so I'm not sure what's going on. I know somebody's being interviewed up in CID.'

He disappeared through a glass-panelled door at the back. Rosa had thought he might invite her to continue the mouse search in his absence.

About three minutes later he returned, accompanied by a plain-clothes officer who introduced himself as Detective Chief Inspector Stanwick.

'We're having a break,' he said. 'Your client said he'd like a cup of coffee before we continued.'

'May I take it he hasn't been charged with anything?'

'Not yet.'

'How am I meant to interpret that?'

He gave her a wisp of a smile. 'As far as I'm concerned "not yet" has only one meaning, namely "not yet".'

'How much longer are you proposing to keep him here?'

'That depends on the co-operation we receive. Why don't you go and talk to him?'

He came round to the front of the counter and Rosa followed him out of a side door and up a flight of stairs.

'I wondered if our paths would cross again,' he remarked as they reached the top. 'I remember you, though I don't expect you remember me.'

Rosa frowned. She didn't like being caught out.

'I recall doing a case in Havenbridge about five years ago. A local councillor had fiddled his expenses. But you weren't the officer in charge.'

'No, that was Detective Inspector Tate, who's now retired. I was his side-kick.' He smiled. 'Being Taffy Tate's number two was quite an experience. He made sure you got all the kicks and none of the kudos.'

'I remember now,' Rosa said. 'You were the officer who arrested my client when he made a panic dash the day before his court appearance. You found him standing on the edge of a cliff.'

'Actually, he was safely back from the edge. He never had any intention of jumping.' He paused in front of a door and opened it. 'You have a visitor, Mr Pickard.'

Adrian was sitting in a sparsely furnished room, staring into a half-drunk cup of coffee which was now covered by a layer of wrinkled skin.

He glanced up and his expression changed. 'Rosa! Thank God you're here.'

'Margaret phoned me and I came as soon as I could.'

'The police know I was following Wells that night and keep asking why I didn't tell them. They then suggested it was because I'd killed him.'

'How did they find out you followed him?'

He grimaced. 'I don't think they did actually know, but they tricked me into admitting it.'

'By making you believe they knew?'

'Yes,' he said forlornly.

No wonder, Rosa reflected, Chief Inspector Stanwick had seemed so relaxed and sure of himself.

'Have they suggested what motive you had?'

'The same as before: that I was following him when he turned and attacked me and I killed him in the course of defending myself.'

'So they're offering you the same soft option again,' Rosa observed.

'But I didn't kill him.' He gave her an imploring look. 'Get me out of this place, Rosa. I have to get back to Margaret. She'll be worried stiff. They can't keep me here, can they?'

'They'll either have to charge you or release you. And if they charge you with manslaughter, I doubt whether they'll object to bail.'

It was cold comfort, but the best she felt able to offer.

A few minutes later the door opened and an officer with a flourishing moustache appeared.

'Chief Inspector Stanwick wonders if your client feels ready to continue the interview?' he said, addressing Rosa.

Before she had time to reply, Adrian had jumped up. 'Yes, let's get it over with,' he said, moving toward the door.

It seemed to Rosa that the police were employing every soft tactic they knew to obtain a confession to manslaughter. It was very different from the psychological hammering her clients usually received in such circumstances. Physical violence was a rarity, but mental pressure could be ruthlessly applied.

When they entered his office, Stanwick got up from behind his desk in the manner of a polite host.

'Well, Mr Pickard,' he remarked, 'have you thought about what I was saying?'

'And what exactly were you saying?' Rosa broke in.

Stanwick looked at her in surprise. 'Didn't your client tell you?'

'I'd still like to hear it from you.'

Stanwick pursed his lips. 'I'm afraid Mr Pickard hasn't been entirely straightforward in his dealings with us. He's shown a certain reluctance to tell us the truth. I told him at the outset that if he would help me, I'd probably be able to help him. I still don't believe he deliberately murdered Wells, though the longer it takes him to be frank about what actually happened, the more I begin to wonder.'

'I understand you think he killed in self-defence?'

'I have suggested that, if that's the truth, the sooner he admits it, the better it will be for him.'

'But it's not the truth and my client denies absolutely that he played any part in Wells' death.'

'I see. In that event, our enquiries will continue and it's more than likely I'll want to interview Mr Pickard again. No need to tell someone as experienced as yourself, Miss Epton, that a plea to manslaughter in a case such as this could result in a nominal penalty. Of course I'm speaking off the record.' Glancing across at Adrian he said, 'That's all for the time being, Mr Pickard. You're free to go. I take it you don't have any plans to leave the country?'

'None.'

'That's all right then. As long as I know where I can find you.'

'I'm not going to abscond, if that's what you mean.'

'Good.'

As they made to leave, Rosa hung back to have a word with Stanwick out of her client's earshot.

'Have you been able to find out what Wells was doing in Greenborough?'

'I don't think there's much doubt about that. He was a burglar on reconnaissance.'

'If that's so, is it likely he'd have drawn attention to himself by creating a disturbance in the post office?'

'He'd drunk too much and it made him truculent. The pathologist found evidence that he'd been drinking.'

Rosa doubted his explanation, but refrained from further comment.

Adrian was silent and withdrawn on the drive back to Greenborough. Rosa thought he was probably not looking forward to explaining himself to Margaret. On arrival he invited her in for a drink, but Rosa declined.

'Thank you for coming to my rescue,' he said in a dispirited voice. He glanced at the windows of his home. 'It looks as if Margaret has already gone to bed. Have a safe journey home, Rosa.' He blew her a quick kiss and walked across the grass verge toward the cottage gate.

Once in the car Rosa inserted a tape into the machine Peter had given her (which was worth almost as much as the car itself) and was immediately soothed by the waltz themes from *Der Rosenkavalier*. Listening to music was an important element in her life. She liked to have lumps brought to her throat and tingles sent up and down her spine and music that didn't do this for her failed in its purpose.

It was just before midnight when she turned into the Kensington street where she had lived since first moving to London. Her heart gave a little jump when she saw Peter's car parked outside her flat. He had his own set of keys and had obviously come round after arriving home and finding her message on his answering machine. A welcome home was just what she needed. The drive back had stirred her adrenalin and though tired, she was no longer sleepy.

She climbed the stairs to her top-floor flat. As she reached her front door, it opened to reveal Peter standing with what she always called one of his oriental smiles. Friendly, but curiously enigmatic.

'How lovely to find you here,' she said, putting her arms round his neck.

He responded by kissing her with the quiet ardour that invariably made her legs go weak.

'Have you had anything to eat?' he asked, after releasing her.

She shook her head. 'Nothing since a hard-boiled egg at lunch.'

'I thought you might be hungry,' he said, 'so I've made some smoked salmon sandwiches.'

'Wonderful!'

'And I've put a bottle of champagne on ice.'

'Even more wonderful!'

'You go and sit down and I'll fetch the food and drink. Then you can tell me about your evening with the sub-postmaster.'

As they ate, Rosa unwound and ceased to protest every time Peter refilled her glass.

'There's something very odd about Adrian,' she said with a sigh. 'I'm quite sure he's still not told me the whole truth.'

'Why don't you have a word with Margaret?'

'It would only worry her and sow doubts in her mind.' She paused. 'I suspect she knows even less about him than I do.'

Peter was silent as he poured the remainder of the champagne into their glasses. Then he said, 'Sooner or later the police are going to charge someone in respect of Wells' death. If it's not Adrian Pickard you can wash your hands of him as a client. On the other hand if it is Adrian, it'll bring matters to a head.'

'I wonder if it'll be as simple as that,' Rosa said in a voice full of doubt.

12

To his mother, Harry Wells had been a good son. He not only supported her financially, if somewhat irregularly, but he would bring her presents which he knew she would like such as a new handbag, a bedside radio and other small luxuries. But the gift she treasured most of all was a cordless telephone which she carried around the house like a child with a favourite doll.

It was about a week after Chief Inspector Stanwick's visit when she was sitting in front of the TV waiting for *Coronation Street* to begin that it suddenly rang. It had been silent all day and she tut-tutted that it chose this particular moment to demand attention.

At first she didn't hear what her caller said. It was a male voice and had an indistinct bubbly quality, as if he was speaking under water.

'I didn't catch your name,' she said.

'I was a good friend of Harry's,' came the reply.

'I'm sorry, but I still don't have your name.'

'Philip.'

She searched her memory, but couldn't recall Harry ever mentioning anyone of that name. Sometimes names of people he had met tripped off his tongue and she didn't make much effort to take them in.

'Philip,' he repeated.

'Not Phil? I believe he once mentioned someone called Phil.'

'That's right, that's me,' the man said quickly. 'Philip, Phil, some call me one, some the other. I thought I'd give you a ring to see how you're coping. Everything all right?'

'How can it be all right with my poor Harry dead? It's been a terrible shock to me.'

'I'm sure. I suppose the police have been to see you?'

'Yes.'

'Asked a lot of questions, did they?'

It was at this point that she decided to be extra careful with what she said to Phil.

'I expect they wanted to know what he was doing in Greenborough?' he went on.

'There was nothing I could tell them.'

'Did you mention your own connection with Greenborough?'

'Who are you? Why are you asking all these questions?'

'I've told you. I was a friend of Harry's.'

'That doesn't give you the right to ask me questions.'

'I didn't mean to upset you. In fact, I was wondering if I might be able to help you.'

'Help me? How?'

'I owed Harry a good turn, so if you need a bit of money, I could let you have some.'

'I don't want your help.'

'No strings attached or anything like that.' He paused. 'You see, I know rather more about Harry than you may think. About what he was doing in Greenborough that day, for example.'

'I don't believe you're Phil at all. You're a reporter.'

'I assure you I'm not that.'

'Well, whatever you are, I've nothing more to say to you. And if you phone me again, I'll tell the police.'

'I'm sure there are lots of things you could tell the police which would interest them.'

She had had enough of her importunate caller and rang off. She felt hot and confused. Moreover, she had missed half of *Coronation Street* and was in no mood to watch the remainder. It had been a most unsettling call, particularly the insinuation that the man with the bubbly voice knew things about her. It was bad enough that Harry had found out details of her past, for as far as she was concerned there were some secrets you took with you to the grave. She would sooner that Harry's death went unavenged than that the past should be raked over.

She felt one of her angina attacks coming on and reached for the bottle of tablets. It was all the fault of her mysterious caller. She knew she must sit absolutely still and think quiet thoughts. In due course, the attack eased and she rested her head against the small pillow which was fixed to the back of her winged chair. It had been another of Harry's thoughtful little gifts. Her mind drifted back to the year 1932 when she had been a girl in Greenborough and Wally Price used to take her out on the pillion of his motorcycle. She could remember clearly the day he was arrested and charged with murder. She had never seen him again, her parents despatching her to an aunt and uncle who lived in Matlock. She had of course read about Wally's trial and had later learnt of his suicide, but his name was never allowed to be mentioned. She had loved Wally, whatever people said about him.

She felt suddenly drained of energy and ready to fall asleep. She reflected drowsily how her adolescent years had been overshadowed by Wally Price's trial and subsequent suicide. And now her own son's violent death had come to haunt her like a curse.

13

'Stay where you are and don't move. You're under arrest.'

Adrian Pickard had been so absorbed in what he was doing that he hadn't heard anyone approach. He gave a convulsive start and dropped the flashlight he had in his hand. The other person now switched on his own more powerful torch and focused its beam on Adrian's face.

'I can explain,' Adrian stammered.

'Save your explanations for the court. You've been caught red-handed.'

The man came closer and Adrian could see he was in police uniform.

'I do assure you, officer, it's not what you think. I'm not a burglar.'

'Then what are you doing breaking into Warren Hall School?'

'I can explain. I'm sure Mr Thurston won't wish to press charges when he hears.'

'Mr Thurston's gone away.'

'I know . . .'

'Of course you know, that's why you chose now to break in.' In a tone of some satisfaction, he added, 'He notified the police he'd be away for a few days and asked us to keep an eye on the place.' He steadied the beam of his torch on Adrian's face. 'You run the post office in Greenborough, don't you?'

'Yes,' Adrian said eagerly. 'I often take a walk in the school grounds.'

'And break into the building?' the officer enquired sarcastically.

'I haven't actually broken in.'

'No? So how did you get in?'

'I got . . . I climbed . . . I came through a pantry window,' Adrian said unhappily. 'But I'm not a burglar.'

'You're giving a very good imitation of one.'

'You can search me, I've not stolen anything.'

'I'll search you all right, but whether or not I find anything, you're still a burglar.' He moved closer. 'Hold out your hands.'

Adrian did so and found himself immediately handcuffed.

'Please believe me,' he said urgently. 'You're making a terrible mistake. Now you know who I am, you must realise I'm not a burglar.'

'Save your breath.'

'What would I be stealing here?'

They were standing in a corridor whose walls were lined with school photographs. Cricket and football teams, as well as the annual ones taken of the whole school each summer term, staff sitting on benches and boys ranged in tiers behind them, with the smallest squatting on the ground in front like tiny smirking Buddhas.

Classrooms led off the corridor, empty and silent as they awaited the new term's onslaught of boys.

There was a sound of footsteps at one end of the corridor.

'You all right?' a voice called out.

'Yeah, I caught him red-handed.'

'Who is it?'

'You can take a look if you want.'

Adrian had already recognised Joe Atherly's voice. He blinked as the officer shone his torch on to his face for Atherly's benefit.

'Huh! I thought it might be him. Postmaster, indeed!'

'Lucky you spotted the light or he'd have got away with whatever he was up to.'

'Always ready to help the police,' Atherly said smugly. 'I knew there shouldn't be no lights showing with Mr Thurston away.' He let out a sudden exclamation. 'Come to think of it, I heard him tell this chap he was going away for a few days. I was standing behind him in the post office when he mentioned it.'

'OK Joe, we'll need to have a statement from you. Meanwhile, I'd better get our burglar friend back to the station and have him charged. It's been a good evening's work.'

'It's crazy to say I'm a burglar. I didn't steal anything,' Adrian protested for the umpteenth time, on each occasion with increased agitation, as he and Rosa faced each other in a small airless room at Havenbridge Magistrates' Court.

'Forget the word,' Rosa said with a sigh. 'All the charge means

80

is that you entered the premises as a trespasser with intent to steal . . .'

'I had no intention of stealing anything.'

'*Or*,' Rosa went on, 'to cause unlawful damage to the building or anything therein.'

'That's absurd.'

'There can't be any doubt that you entered as a trespasser,' she said firmly.

'I can explain that.'

'They've also stuck on a charge of causing malicious damage,' she went on. 'The catch on the pantry window was forced.'

'Forced, indeed! It didn't need any forcing. It almost fell off at the first gentle push.'

'I think it's time you faced the reality of your situation. How are the postal authorities going to react to your being charged with a criminal offence?'

He sagged and let out a small groan. 'It's awful. Heaven knows how I'm going to explain it all to Margaret.'

At that moment an usher stuck his head round the door. 'You'll be on in a couple of minutes,' he said.

Adrian followed Rosa out of the interview room with all the enthusiasm of a small boy being delivered to a new school. The two lay magistrates had already taken their seats on the bench and Detective Chief Inspector Stanwick gave Rosa a brief nod as they entered the courtroom. It was a modern one with tip-up seats that made distracting noises when sat on and which sprang noisily back when released. Rosa had come across the type of seat before and felt they must have been designed by a manufacturer of party jokes.

Adrian was ushered into the small dock, where he stood trying to look invisible. The clerk read out the two charges and glanced at Rosa.

'As you're aware, Miss Epton, this court has jurisdiction to try both these charges. If your client elects trial here, are you ready to proceed with the case today?'

'I'm asking for a remand on bail, your worships, as I've not yet had time to take proper instructions from my client, who was only arrested and charged last night.'

A pale, rather haunted-looking young man at the further end of the solicitors' seats rose and said that the Crown Prosecution

Service had no objection to a remand on bail. If anything, his tone was one of relief. As Rosa was well aware, representatives of the CPS were liable to receive a hammering from every quarter these days, so that a case adjourned could be a roasting deferred.

It took the magistrates less than a minute to remand Adrian on bail for six weeks.

As Rosa was leaving court, Stanwick fell in beside her.

'I should be interested to know what your client was up to last night,' he remarked. 'But I suppose I shall have to wait.'

Rosa felt inclined to say that he couldn't be more interested than she was, but gave him a long-suffering smile instead.

'Where can we talk?' Rosa said, as she and Adrian left the building. 'Somewhere we're not known and won't be overheard.'

Adrian shook his head with a deflated expression. 'I can't think of anywhere. It's awful. Everyone in Greenborough will know by now. I'll have to hide.'

'Running away's not going to help,' Rosa said brutally. 'In fact, it'll make things worse. Incidentally, does Margaret know you're at court this morning?'

'I told her I had to see the district postmaster in Havenbridge.'

'You'll have to tell her the truth some time. What happened when you got home last night after the police had released you?'

'She was asleep and didn't wake up.' He gave Rosa a rueful look. 'Recently I've been sleeping in the spare room as she says I snore.'

Rosa could see this as one cloud with a silver lining.

'There's a small roadside café on the outskirts of Havenbridge,' he said suddenly. 'We could go there, though their coffee isn't very good.'

'We're not going for the coffee,' Rosa said. 'We're going so that you can start telling me the truth.'

14

Rosa watched him bringing two cups of coffee over to their table. The café was empty apart from a leather-clad motorcyclist and his girl-friend.

Adrian put the coffee down. 'I can't remember, do you take sugar?'

Rosa shook her head.

'Is there enough milk in yours?'

This time she nodded.

'I'm afraid I've slopped some into the saucer.'

'Stop prevaricating and tell me what you were doing at Warren Hall School last night?'

'I definitely didn't go there to steal.'

'So?'

He plucked nervously at his lower lip. Then with a deep sigh, he said, 'I wanted to examine one of the school photographs to see if . . . if I could identify my father. I think he was a boy at the school, but I'm not certain.'

Rosa frowned. 'Wasn't there an easier way to find out? Presumably they have records and could tell you whether there was ever a boy named Pickard there.'

'If my father was there, it wouldn't have been as Pickard. It would have been as Willett. Stephen Willett.'

'That's the name of the boy who disappeared and was believed to have been murdered?'

'Yes.'

'And did you recognise your father in any of the photographs?'

'I didn't have time to look properly before the police came. Joe Atherly had seen my torch shining and had alerted them.'

'But you're not absolutely certain your father went to Warren Hall?'

'No. I know he attended a prep school in this area and by a process of elimination I think it was Warren Hall.'

'What makes you believe his name was Willett in those days?'

Adrian gave a despairing shrug. 'I think Margaret told you I never knew my mother. She ran off with a GI soon after I was born and settled in America. As far as my father was concerned, she was dead.'

'What name did your father go by at that time?'

'Edward Pickard. He brought me up himself. We were forever on the move, usually keeping one step ahead of various local authorities who didn't approve of a man with a small boy in tow. And then when I was ten he was killed in a car accident and I found myself alone in the world. I was put out to foster parents until I felt old enough to fight my own battles and I just took off.'

'Did you keep in touch with your foster parents?'

'I was with three different lots and didn't get on with any of them. I used to run away, be picked up by the police and so it would go on. When I was sixteen, I stowed away on a cargo ship and ended up in Singapore. An English lady, called Miss Ingram, who'd lived there all her life, befriended me. She was very musical and gave me piano lessons. I thoroughly enjoyed playing and became quite proficient, but Miss Ingram died suddenly and I was on my own again. I managed to get a job playing the piano in a bar and I eventually worked my way back to England.'

'You haven't explained why you believe your father may have been Stephen Willett,' Rosa broke in. It was a vital question and the answer could be crucial to his defence. Her intuition told her it was also relevant in some way to Harry Wells' death.

'Just various straws in the wind,' he said with a distant expression. 'Nothing dramatic like Paul's experience on the road to Damascus. Just straws over several years.' He shook himself like a dog that has woken up and slowly fixed Rosa with a frowning stare. 'Do you remember the first time we met and I told you I hadn't married Margaret for her money? Do you still believe that?'

'You're here to answer my questions,' she said. 'What were these so-called straws in the wind?'

He nodded slowly. 'I suppose I must have been about three or four when it dawned on me that most children had mothers and I didn't. When I asked my father why, he said she had run away and disappeared. I accepted this, but a year or two later when I discovered about grandparents and asked my father if I had any, and if so where they were, he replied that little boys who asked too many questions had their tongues cut out. That shut me up. I was curious, but not that curious, and anyway there were lots of other things to think about. My father taught me to read and write and I considered myself lucky not to have to go to school. He was always mysterious about his past, but on one occasion he did say he'd been to a school which he referred to as W.H.'

'Warren Hall?'

'That's my guess.'

'Did you ever ask him where he spent the school holidays?'

'No, but he once spoke of a big house in the country and an old man who lived there. Looking back, I realise he'd not had much education himself and yet there was a certain refinement about him. He had breeding, though I couldn't have put it in those words at the time.'

'Did he tell you what he did during the war?'

'Oh, yes. He served in the army in the Western Desert and ended up as a sergeant in a tank regiment. He used to tell me a lot of stories about the war, which I found enthralling. I think his time in the army was probably the happiest of his life.'

'Have you checked army records?'

'Yes. There was a Sergeant Edward Pickard who served in the Royal Tank Corps.'

'I wonder if there's any record of a Stephen Willett at that time?' Rosa said thoughtfully.

'Not one that fits my father. I used to spend most of my time when I wasn't at sea checking aspects of my father's background. As the years went by it became more and more of a challenge to find out all I could. Then not long ago I was glancing through a Sunday newspaper supplement which had pages of advertisements for boys' prep schools and saw the name Warren Hall School at Greenborough. I remembered my father referring to his school by the initials W.H. Then not long after that I saw the name of Sir Denzil Cuckfield in connection with some business deal and recalled how, not long before my father died, I'd been saying I didn't like the name Adrian, and he said I should be thankful I wasn't called Denzil. It was a name I'd never even heard of.'

'Is that the sum total of the straws?' Rosa enquired.

'Not quite. I was a reasonably sensitive child, particularly to atmospheres created by adults, and I often had the feeling my father was brooding over something that had happened in his life. Something he would sooner forget, but which wouldn't go away.'

'Did you ever tax him about it?'

'Only once and he told me pretty sharply I was imagining things and to shut up.'

Rosa was thoughtful for a while. 'Of course if he allowed a man to stand trial for his murder when all along he was alive and well, his conscience may well have bothered him, even if he was only eleven years old at the time it happened. No point in speculating what your father's reaction would have been if Price had faced execution . . .'

'Just to round off the story,' Adrian went on after a sombre pause, 'I'd decided several months before I met Margaret that I wanted a change of direction in my life. I'd always seen myself running a village store. It offered the sort of stability I'd lacked as a ship's entertainer and I'd saved money with that end in view. Then Margaret and I met and decided we would throw in our lot together. Quite fortuitously I read that Greenborough sub post office was up for sale. I didn't disclose my special interest in the village to Margaret, but we came and looked things over and well, you know the rest. Since we arrived I've made further efforts to unravel the past and seem to have landed myself in something of a mess.'

'It's a great pity you didn't seek an opportunity to take a legitimate look at the school photographs, instead of breaking in and getting charged with burglary.'

'That's being wise after the event, Rosa. A legitimate look, as you put it, would have meant telling Bruce Thurston why I wanted to examine school groups of nearly sixty years ago. And that could have opened up a whole new can of worms.'

Rosa recognised the force of this, but didn't see an alternative if the matter was to be resolved.

'Supposing I write to Mr Thurston and explain what you were doing and ask if I may accompany you on a visit to look at the photographs? He'll hardly refuse.'

'You mean tell him that I think my father may have been the missing Stephen Willett of all those years ago?' Adrian asked in a startled tone.

'Why not? There's nothing to be ashamed of in your quest for the truth.'

'But think of the possible repercussions.'

'If you can't find a boy in any of the photographs who resembles your father, that'll be an end of the matter. And, personally, I think that's the most likely outcome.'

'But if I do? My father had one of those faces you take with you through life. I'd reckon being able to pick him out at any age.'

'I'll need to think about it,' Rosa said. 'I'm not sure we'd be able to keep the information to ourselves.'

'You mean, tell the press?' Adrian said aghast.

'It would certainly give them a field day. But what I had in mind was to inform the Home Office or the Registrar of Births, Deaths and Marriages. The Home Office because they may still have papers relating to Price's trial for murder and the Registrar because his records will need straightening out.' Her brow furrowed in thought as she stared across the cheerless scene. 'Now that you don't have to return to court for six weeks, there's no immediate urgency to examine the school groups and it may be better to await events.'

'You mean wait and see whether they charge me with manslaughter?'

'Whether they charge anybody in respect of Wells' death.'

'Do you think this absurd burglary charge will make the police more suspicious of me?'

'I'm afraid so. If they believe you killed Harry Wells, they'll probably think there's some connection between that and the burglary, even if they don't know what. We'll just have to await developments. Meanwhile, I suggest you maintain a low profile.'

'What am I going to tell Margaret?'

'You might try the truth.'

'Could you . . .'

'Definitely not. It's your problem, Adrian, and doesn't fall within my remit as your legal representative.'

A few minutes later they got into their separate cars, Rosa to drive back to London and Adrian to return to Greenborough and a wife who might want to know how he had got on with the district postmaster.

Rosa for her part decided it was time to begin making a few enquiries of her own. Adrian must have been very troubled to act so rashly, and she still didn't know all the reasons why. By the time she reached her office that afternoon, she knew exactly where she would start.

15

'You look tired, Martin,' Lady Cuckfield said to her son when he arrived for Sunday lunch two days later.

He had phoned on Friday evening to propose himself, saying that his wife was taking the children to visit their maternal grandparents for the weekend, but that he couldn't spare the time to go. He also mentioned that he didn't wish to upset his father by staying away. His mother never minded when he came on his own, for she didn't particularly care for her daughter-in-law and found her grandchildren tiring. Sylvia, Martin's wife, was intensely ambitious for her husband – in many ways the perfect wife for an up-and-coming politician.

'I *am* tired,' he said. 'I'm under a lot of pressure at the moment.' He glanced around the hall. 'How's father?'

Joyce Cuckfield looked furtively over her shoulder. 'He went upstairs to change his shoes. He'll be down in a moment. I'm worried about him, Martin. He's been different since the death of this man Wells.'

'In what way?'

'It seems to prey on his mind.'

'I can't think why it should, unless he knows something.' He paused and went on, 'When I spoke to him on the phone two evenings ago, he mentioned the trouble the new postmaster had got into. What on earth was the man doing breaking into Warren Hall?'

'I hear your father coming now,' his mother said hurriedly.

'Don't look so worried, mother,' he remarked.

He was aware, however, that his mother had been a worrier all her life. A worry removed was immediately replaced by a fresh one.

'Thought I heard your car,' Sir Denzil said as he came downstairs. 'Extraordinary things have been happening since you were last here.'

'So I gather.'

'Let's go into the drawing room and have a drink before lunch.'

'I think I'd better go and see how things are progressing in the kitchen,' Lady Cuckfield said with a quick, anxious smile.

'Yes, you go and do that,' her husband retorted in a dismissive tone.

'Are the police any closer to charging someone with Harry Wells' death?' Martin asked when he and his father were seated with a glass of sherry each. Sherry was part of the Sunday ritual; on other days of the week Sir Denzil would have a pink gin before lunch. Lady Cuckfield never partook of more than a thimbleful of anything alcoholic.

'With luck they'll soon be in a position to charge Pickard. I have the impression they just need a bit more evidence.'

'In my view, it'd be better if the crime remained unsolved,' Martin said stiffly.

His father looked at him in surprise. 'I thought you were a law and order man.'

'I am, but I still believe there are some cases where a public trial can result in more harm than good. By all accounts, Harry Wells was a fairly worthless member of society and I can't help feeling that a trial arising out of his death could open old wounds.'

'Old wounds, eh?' his father said with a cocked eyebrow. 'Certainly don't believe in opening them unless they happen to be an enemy's old wounds. Smite your enemy hip and thigh, that's my motto.'

Martin gave his father a curious look, but said nothing.

'Let me give you a refill,' Sir Denzil remarked, picking up the sherry decanter.

'Have the police any idea what Wells was doing in the village?' Martin asked, holding out his glass.

'They think he was on a recce for a burglary. He went into the pub midday and had too much to drink which caused him to become obstreporous in the post office, as a result of which Pickard threw him out. Thereafter nobody seems to have seen him until Atherly found him face down in the stream.'

'How did he get here?'

'He had a ramshackle van, which was found parked near the copse.' He gave his son a hard stare. 'I thought you knew all this.'

'You've probably told me before, but I've had so many things on my mind, I'm not sure what I've heard.' He returned his father's stare. 'You're not specially worried about Wells' death, are you?'

'Worried? Why should I be worried?'

'I got the impression it was on your mind.'

'I don't know where you got that idea from. It's your mother who's been listening to village gossip and speculating over what happened.'

'I imagine you've discussed the case together?'

'As you should know by now, I don't indulge in tittle tattle.'

Martin was silent for a minute, then said, 'I'd like to ask you one question, father. Do you think Wells' death was in any way connected with what happened in the early thirties when a boy disappeared from Warren Hall?'

'Of course not. I know there are rumours circulating to that effect, but they're pure fantasy.'

'What makes you so sure?'

'I was a boy at Warren Hall at the time.'

'I know you were, but that doesn't answer my question.'

'If I may say so, it was a damned silly question.' He gulped down the remains of his sherry and made a face. 'Don't know why I drink this stuff. Now let's go into lunch and talk about something more interesting.'

Martin realised from his father's tone that any attempt to press him further would result in his stalking from the room. And he didn't wish to make things more difficult for his mother.

He followed his father across the hall and into the dining-room. Though the table was laid, there was no sign of any food. Sir Denzil turned round.

'Where's lunch?' he shouted in the direction of the door that led to the kitchen area.

A moment later his wife appeared, looking mildly flustered.

'It'll be a further five minutes,' she said. 'Go and have another glass of sherry.'

'The new couple are useless,' Sir Denzil told his son. 'They've hardly got half a dozen words of English between them. The man's an oaf and his wife's a slut. God knows how your mother came to engage them! You could tell at a glance they wouldn't be any good.' He looked impatiently about him. 'We might as well sit down and wait for the food to arrive. You don't want any more sherry, do you?' Martin shook his head and his father went on, 'I was reading in the paper that your minister may be dropped from the government. Any truth in that?'

'I've no idea.'

'Being loyal, or discreet, or both?' his father enquired. 'He's never struck me as a very dynamic chap.'

'He's a very nice man.'

'That doesn't make him a good minister. To succeed in politics, you need to have a touch of steel.' He gave his son a sharp look. 'Thank goodness you have that quality.'

Before Martin could reply, Lady Cuckfield entered the dining room carrying a tray. She was followed by the male half of the newly engaged couple pushing a trolley.

'Sorry lunch is late,' she said breathlessly.

Sir Denzil made a growling noise while Martin went to help unload the trolley.

'You didn't tell me Joe Atherly was working here this morning,' she went on, addressing her husband.

'What are you talking about?' Sir Denzil asked testily.

'I saw him in the orchard when I went to the back door just now.'

'What was he doing?'

'I couldn't see. I only caught sight of the top of his head. Perhaps he was picking up a few windfalls, though . . .'

'Though what?' Sir Denzil asked with an angry frown.

'He seemed more interested in the house than anything. He kept peering in this direction.'

'He has no right to trespass.'

'I'm sure he didn't mean any harm,' Martin said quickly.

Lunch had got off to a bad start and nothing happened to alleviate the strained, chilly atmosphere which had settled over the dining room like an unfriendly sea mist.

16

Bruce Thurston arrived home at lunchtime that same Sunday. He had been spending a few days at a cottage he owned in Wales when he received news of the break-in at the school. Joe Atherly had been the first to call him, with the police phoning several hours later.

'Thought I'd let you know that fellow Pickard was caught burgling the school last night,' Joe had said. 'I spotted a light and rang the police. They caught Pickard red-handed.'

'What had he stolen?'

'He hadn't got that far. I was too quick for him.'

'Well, thanks, Joe, for such a display of public-spiritedness.' The note of irony was entirely lost on Atherly.

'That's all right. By the way, I was able to tell the police where you were. I said I knew you had a cottage in Wales. I later got the number from directory enquiries.'

When later the police called to give him the same information, Bruce Thurston thanked them and said he would return home at once. He was more than curious to know what Adrian Pickard had been up to. Joe Atherly, too. Somehow the public-spirited citizen image didn't become him.

Parents were a conservative breed where their sons' education in the private sector was concerned and Warren Hall was currently going through an especially difficult period with rising costs and falling numbers. There was also his own personal crisis involving a brief fling with a young P.E. teacher, which had resulted in his wife moving out. The official story was that she had gone to look after a stricken parent and hoped to be back by next term. But it wasn't the sort of story that could be easily perpetuated, and if a scandal broke the school could once again suffer. It had suffered and survived a scandal of fifty years before, which was still within the living memory of various people. But could the school survive another?

It was with these thoughts swirling around his head that he returned to Greenborough that Sunday.

He had driven non-stop and was hungry by the time he arrived home. He and his wife (when she was there) lived on a floor of the main house that had been converted into a self-contained flat, though they took most of their meals in the main dining hall during term time.

He let himself in through a side door which was the regular way in and out during the holidays, the massive front door of the house being kept locked and bolted while staff and boys were away. A corridor of green and white tiles led to the classrooms. Half-way along, a carpeted staircase led up to the headmaster's private quarters. A sign at the bottom said 'PRIVATE' to deter boys from exploring an area which was out of bounds except by invitation.

He reached the top of the staircase and let out a sigh. He always found the school building strangely oppressive when it was deserted. For over ninety years it had grown used to the raucous noise created by successive generations of schoolboys. Silence didn't become it and today that silence seemed to have a particularly eerie quality about it.

He closed the door of the private quarters behind him, tossed his bag into the bedroom and headed for the kitchen. Armed with a can of beer and a ham sandwich he sat down at the table in the dining alcove.

He was wondering what exactly he was going to do now that he had returned, when the telephone rang. There was an extension fixed to the kitchen wall and he frowned at it. It was as if somebody had seen him return and knew he was there. He slid along the bench seat and reached for the phone.

'That you, Mr Thurston?' a familiar voice enquired. 'It's Joe Atherly. I think we ought to meet.'

'I'll get in touch with you in the course of the week, Joe.'

'I think we ought to meet this evening.'

'Why do you want to see me?'

'I'll tell you when we meet.'

'I can't manage this evening. It won't be convenient.'

'I'll come up to the school around ten o'clock. It's important.'

'I shall be out.'

'See you at ten,' Joe said, and rang off leaving Thurston feeling he'd been talking to a stone wall. It had been a disconcerting conversation and had done nothing to improve the headmaster's tetchy mood.

He finished his sandwich and on the spur of the moment reached once more for the phone and dialled a number.

'Is that Mrs Pickard?' he asked when a female voice answered.

'It is.'

'This is Bruce Thurston. May I speak to your husband please?'

'I'm afraid he's out. Can I give him a message?'

'Don't worry, I'll try and catch him later.'

'Very well.'

He had the impression he had woken Margaret Pickard from a siesta. After washing up his plate and beer mug, he left the kitchen and retraced his steps through the echoing corridors of the empty building.

He would go out. Anything was better than spending a Sunday afternoon shut away in his deserted school – especially after Joe Atherly's disquieting phone call.

Gwen Atherly woke with a start. It was dark outside, but the television was on and illuminated the room with a ghostly light. She screwed up her eyes to try and see the time by her watch. It took her several seconds to make out the position of the hands. Eventually, she decided it was a few minutes after nine o'clock. It wasn't unusual for her to fall asleep in front of the telly, particularly if she'd had a bad night. Her arthritis ensured she never had a really good one. It was merely a question of the degree of sleeplessness she had endured.

Joe wasn't in and had presumably returned to the pub. Nothing unusual about that either. On Sundays he invariably went for a lunchtime drink and again in the evening unless there was something special on telly he wanted to watch, such as a football match.

She heaved herself out of her chair and hobbled into the kitchen. Joe would want some supper when he came in and she was ready to eat now. As she set about making some cheese and pickle sandwiches, she thanked the Almighty for having guided somebody to invent sliced bread. Cutting a loaf was now beyond her gnarled hands. She was constantly offering up small prayers of thanks to God for looking after her needs. It was all very well for Joe to scoff, but her faith remained the core of her existence.

She returned to their small front parlour with her sandwich and a mug of hot chocolate, which she wasn't supposed to drink. But there wasn't much point to life if you couldn't occasionally indulge yourself at her age. She was seventy, six years younger than Joe, and the cottage in which they now lived had once been occupied by her parents.

She could remember the present headmaster's grandfather when he had been headmaster of Warren Hall. To a somewhat timid, shy girl he had been an alarming figure whom she did her best to avoid.

She had been twelve when Stephen Willett disappeared from the school and she clearly remembered the excitement it generated. Nobody had any doubt that he had been murdered and that Wally Price was the guilty party. There were those who felt that Joe had behaved shabbily by putting the police on to Wally's tracks. There had been no need, they said, for Joe to have opened his mouth so quickly. Greenborough was a close village community in those days and grassing wasn't considered a respectable option.

But Joe had managed to live down the shame of giving evidence for the prosecution at Wally's trial, though never forgiven by Wally himself.

Gwen recalled how desperately sorry she had felt for Norma Kirk, the girl whom Wally had been courting at the time of his arrest. She had vanished from the village overnight. Gwen herself had been too young to attract Wally's attention and had been faintly resentful of the fact.

She glanced at the clock and pulled a face. Joe was later than usual which meant he would almost certainly be the worse for wear when he came in. Drink was apt to make him morose, which, she supposed, was better than being truculent and aggressive. She would give him another half-hour and then get herself to bed, a slow and painful process with her various joints protesting at every move.

She woke up in the night and realised Joe wasn't in the room. He had probably fallen asleep downstairs. It wouldn't be the first time.

But morning came and with it the discovery that Joe had still not returned home. As she drank her first cup of tea of the day, Gwen wondered what she should do. An obvious starting point was to call Arthur Flack, the local publican, and ask him what time Joe had left his premises the previous evening.

When Flack informed her that Joe had not put in an appearance after his midday visit, she decided to get in touch with the police.

Twenty-four hours after Joe had left home that Sunday, there was still no sign of him. Hospitals had been checked and all the ditches and hedgerows in the vicinity of Greenborough had been searched.

It was at that point that his disappearance became a criminal investigation and landed fairly and squarely on Chief Inspector Stanwick's desk.

17

Rosa was unaware of Joe Atherly's disappearance when she set off to visit Mrs Wells in Woolwich on Monday afternoon.

She had given Ben such clues as she had, namely a widow named Wells in her seventies whose youngest son, Harry, had died a violent death in Greenborough, and asked him to try and find out her address.

'No problem, Miss E,' Ben replied cheerfully and twenty-four hours later came up with the information.

'I think the lady you want, Miss E, is a Mrs Norma Wells of 28 Volga Close, Woolwich,' he reported. 'She's not in good health and relies a good deal on neighbours. She refuses to go into a home and says she's staying put until they take her out in a box.'

'You've done brilliantly, Ben. Many thanks.'

'No problem, Miss E.'

Rosa had also undertaken some research of her own and had spent an afternoon in the British Museum Newspaper Library reading accounts of Walter Price's trial for murder.

It was around three thirty p.m. when she arrived outside 28 Volga Close. She locked her car and approached the front door. It opened before she had time to press the bell. A middle-aged woman in a floral pinafore confronted her.

'Is Mrs Wells in?' Rosa asked with a tentative smile.

'She may be. Who are you?'

'My name's Rosa Epton and I'm a solicitor. I'd very much like to have a word with Mrs Wells. It's about her son's death.'

The woman looked her up and down with marked suspicion, then turned and went back inside the house. Rosa heard the woman who had opened the door say, 'She looks all right. Shall I let her in?' A few moments later she reappeared. 'Yes, all right, come in.' Lowering her voice she went on, 'She gets dizzy spells, but as long as you don't upset her, she should be all right. Her pills are on the table beside her if she needs one.'

Rosa followed the woman into the front room where Mrs Wells was sitting with a tartan rug over her knees. She eyed Rosa with interest.

'You don't look like a solicitor,' she remarked.

Rosa smiled. 'I'll take that as a compliment,' she said.

'You're too pretty,' Mrs Wells went on.

'Thank you,' Rosa replied, this time with a friendly laugh. 'There are lots of girls practising as lawyers these days.'

'I've seen them on telly.'

'They exist in real life, too.'

'Why have you come to see me, Miss . . .?'

'Please call me Rosa. I've come because I believe you may be the only person who can answer certain questions. Am I right in thinking you grew up in Greenborough and that your original name was Norma Kirk?'

'What's the point of these questions?'

'They could have a bearing on your son's death.'

She shook her head vigorously. 'No. No.'

'Why are you so sure?'

'Because I am sure.'

'Why do you think Harry was killed then?'

'He was a good son, but he had some bad friends.'

'Do you remember Wally Price?'

She shot Rosa a fierce, resentful look. 'What do you know about Wally? He's been dead nearly sixty years.'

'I know.'

'May his soul rest in peace.'

'Were you and Wally in love with each other, Mrs Wells?'

She put up a hand as if to ward off the question.

'It's all so long ago and you're confusing me with your questions. And now my Harry's gone, too.'

'I'm sorry if I've upset you, Mrs Wells. Can I fetch you anything?'

Mrs Wells appeared not to be listening and went on, 'Everything's upsetting me these days. There was that man who phoned and pretended to be a friend of Harry's, but he wasn't.'

'What man was that?' Rosa asked with quickened interest.

'Like I said, pretending to be a friend of Harry's and trying to get information out of me.'

'What was his name?'

'Said he was Philip, but Harry had never mentioned anyone called Philip. He did once know someone named Phil and this man then pretended to be Phil. Whoever he was, I wasn't going to talk to him. His voice sounded funny, too. All bubbly like.'

'Do you mean he was drunk?'

'No, it was as though he was under water.'

'It could have been a reporter,' Rosa remarked. 'They get up to all sorts of tricks when they're trying to dig out information.'

Mrs Wells gave Rosa a sudden, suspicious stare. 'You're not a reporter, are you?'

'No, I've told you, I'm a solicitor.'

'You could be pretending to be a solicitor.'

'I promise you I'm not.' She got up and said with a friendly smile, 'Why don't I make some tea?'

'I could do with a cuppa.'

When Rosa returned to the front room with a tray of tea things a few minutes later she thought Mrs Wells had fallen asleep, but at the first rattle of cup on saucer her eyes snapped open.

'Whose solicitor are you?' she asked suddenly.

'I represent someone called Adrian Pickard. He runs the post office at Greenborough.'

'Did he kill Harry?'

'I'm quite sure he didn't.'

'If he did, I hope he's found guilty.'

'I'm certain he didn't. He hasn't even been charged.' Rosa paused, then said, 'Does the name Stephen Willett mean anything to you?'

'He was the boy . . .'

'Yes?'

'Nothing.'

'What boy were you thinking of?'

'Just a boy.'

'He was the boy Wally Price was accused of murdering.'

'I don't remember. I could do with another cup of tea.'

Rosa poured it for her and sat down again. 'Do you remember the Cuckfield family? They still own Greenborough Court. The present Sir Denzil was a boy at Warren Hall when you were a girl in the village.'

She turned away. 'I don't remember,' she muttered.

Rosa decided she had learnt as much as she was likely to: nothing was going to persuade the old lady to reveal secrets which were locked away in her heart.

She carried the tea tray back to the kitchen and washed the cups and saucers. When she returned to the front room she found Mrs Wells staring at a framed photograph on the mantelpiece.

'Is that Harry?'

The old lady nodded vaguely, but her mind had obviously retreated into the past and was reliving memories that would never leave her.

Rosa thanked Mrs Wells for her kindness in talking to her and said she hoped to see her again. Norma Wells might now be on the sidelines, but it was Rosa's belief that, wittingly or otherwise, she held the clue to recent events in Greenborough.

18

Peter Chen had been in Vancouver visiting one of his Hong Kong clients who had moved his family and fortune there in advance of 1997 and Rosa hadn't seen him for the best part of a week, though he called her almost every night. But he had arrived home that day and was coming to dinner, and Rosa found herself looking forward to seeing him again with all the eagerness of a new bride.

She had prepared a liver and bacon casserole which she knew he liked and made a fresh fruit salad, so that their meal was already looked after.

She called in at the office on her return from Woolwich to find out if there had been any dramas or emergencies during her absence. Fortunately, there had been neither and Stephanie reported that the afternoon had been surprisingly peaceful.

On arrival home she put the casserole in the oven after adding a drop more red wine to it. She also gave the fruit salad a good stir before returning it to the refrigerator. After which she had a bath and put on fresh clothes.

Peter, who was always slavishly punctual, arrived on the dot of seven forty-five.

'Little Rosa,' he exclaimed, flinging wide his arms, when she opened the front door. She skipped into his embrace and for a while they kissed in silence. 'You look stunning and smell delicious,' he said when they broke apart.

'I could say the same about you,' Rosa remarked with an affectionate smile.

'It's my new "Big Man" aftershave.'

'Not to mention a new shirt and sweater,' she said.

He always managed to look as if he had been freshly unwrapped when they spent an evening together.

They went into her small living room where she had put out a tray of drinks, which she did only for special occasions. She poured him a malt whisky and added Malvern water and gave herself a Campari and orange juice.

Reaching into his trouser pocket, he produced a small package.

'It's not genuine,' he said hastily, as she began to unwrap it. 'Just genuine fake made in Taiwan.'

'It's beautiful, Peter,' she said, gazing at the small bejewelled gold egg in the palm of her hand.

'Forget Fabergé and like it for itself,' Peter said, pleased with her reaction. 'The gold and the jewels are genuine.'

Rosa leaned forward and kissed him. 'I don't deserve it.'

'I disagree. Now tell me what's been happening in Greenborough.'

'First, tell me about Vancouver.'

'Lots of water, lots of mountains and lots of Chinese. Oh, and some Canadians, too. Now tell me about you and Greenborough.'

He listened intently while Rosa regaled him with details of what had happened during his absence.

'What an incredible story,' he observed when she finished telling him of Adrian Pickard's latest exploits at Warren Hall. 'Do you believe him?'

'I can't think he invented it.'

'But you've not yet told the police why he broke in?'

'No, but I'll have to decide fairly soon whether to use it as his defence to the burglary charge.'

'It'll create a sensation,' Peter remarked.

'That's what I'm afraid of. It'll open a Pandora's box from which anything may pop out.'

'I seem to remember that all the ills of human life escaped from the original one.'

'It's the unknown elements I'm worried about.'

'Have you been in touch with Adrian since the day he appeared in court?'

'No.' Rosa paused. 'I almost added, thank goodness.'

'I wonder if he's told Margaret yet.'

'I doubt it. And that only complicates matters.' She sighed. 'Representing a member of one's family in a professional capacity can be a recipe for disaster.' She took hold of Peter's hand. 'Let's go and eat.'

Over their meal she told him of her visit to Woolwich.

'It sounds as if you were trying to prise open another Pandora's box,' Peter remarked.

Rosa smiled. 'No chance with Mrs Wells sitting firmly on it.'

'She may have opened it for the police.'

'I very much doubt it. I'd be surprised if they learnt any more from her than I did. If as much.'

'What's her secret?'

'At the moment I can only speculate, but I intend to find out.' She was about to go on, but was interrupted by the telephone. 'Cross your fingers and hope it's not Adrian,' she said.

'Shall I answer it and say you're out?'

'I'd better see who it is. After all, Adrian isn't the only person who calls me.'

'Tell whoever it is that you can only talk for half a minute at the most. Tell them,' Peter added as Rosa reached the door, 'that you're making meringues and they've reached a critical stage.'

Soon after she and Peter had first met, Rosa had used this as an excuse not to linger on the phone when he had called her on one occasion. From time to time he liked to remind her of it.

'Oh, hello, Adrian,' he heard her say. There followed a sequence of 'I see's' and 'yes, go on's'. Peter, meanwhile, poured

101

himself another glass of wine and stationed the bottle beside him.

'What's happened now?' he asked, when she eventually returned to the kitchen.

'The police have been questioning Adrian again. Not only Adrian, but most of the village. It seems that Joe Atherly has gone missing and they think something's happened to him.'

'That he's dead?'

'That's the presumption. They've been scouring the surrounding countryside this afternoon but without success. Apparently they had a search party of volunteers out with the police and Adrian took part.'

'When did he disappear?'

'It seems he went out between four and five yesterday afternoon and hasn't been seen since. He didn't tell his wife where he was going, but she formed the impression he was going to meet somebody. He'd been in the pub midday and his wife assumed he'd gone back there in the evening. But he didn't.'

'It's possible he had a heart attack and collapsed in a ditch or behind a hedge.'

'That's why they've had a search party out looking for him.'

'If he was taken suddenly ill he may have sought shelter somewhere under cover.'

'You make him sound like a missing kitten, but I suppose it's a possibility. I'd have thought, however, that if you had any warning of an attack, you'd make for the nearest house and ask for help.'

'Does he want you to go and hold his hand?'

'I think he'd be quite glad if I did.'

'But what on earth could you do?'

'Nothing. I made that clear before he could make the suggestion. Everything now depends on the discovery of Joe Atherly, dead or alive.'

'I can't see him turning up alive.'

'Nor can I,' Rosa said. 'And if Atherly's been murdered it has to be connected with Harry Wells' death and that takes us back to 1932. Wells' mother was Wally Price's girl-friend and Joe Atherly was a witness at Wally's trial.' She frowned and went on, 'That must be significant, if I could only work out how.'

'Forget them all,' Peter said, pushing back his chair. 'I'll make the coffee and you unplug the telephone.'

'That sounds like a good idea,' Rosa said.

'I've got an even better one,' he replied, leaning over and kissing her behind the ear.

19

Miss Spurling had been the matron at Warren Hall for seven years. She was an efficient, even formidable woman in mid-life who kept the junior staff in their place and stood no nonsense from the boys. She had jet black hair, which she kept short, and a moustache, which gave rise to endless jokes and horror stories among the boys.

She occupied a small bed-sitting room at the top of the house which was out of bounds to everyone save one of the cleaners.

Normally she returned to the school two or three days before each term began, having spent the holidays with an aged aunt who lived in Lincoln. Apart from her moustache, she was remembered by the boys for her cycling. Whenever she went out, it would be on her bicycle, whether to the village or for an invigorating fifteen-mile ride.

She arrived back at the school for the start of the new term on the Tuesday after Joe Atherly's disappearance. This was a day earlier than she would normally have been expected and she had tried to phone the headmaster to tell him, but could get no reply. Not that this bothered her, for she could be self-sufficient with facilities for simple cooking provided in a pantry along the corridor.

The reason for her early return was to arrange for a puncture in the rear tyre of her bicycle to be repaired. It had occurred when she was cycling back to school two days after the summer term had ended and the evening before she was due to go to her aunt. Being a person who neither offered favours nor asked them, she left the bicycle in a shed used for storing sports equipment, covering it with an old tarpaulin.

She had missed it while she was staying in Lincoln, but had eventually hired an inferior one to get around on.

The school appeared deserted when she arrived back around five o'clock that Tuesday afternoon. She noticed that Mr Thurston's car was missing from its usual place and assumed he was out. She wondered whether Mrs Thurston had returned to the fold. As far as she was concerned the headmaster was undeserving of any sympathy. Men of his age and position should know better than to have flings with younger women.

A glance inside the kitchen told her that Mrs Edwards, the cook, hadn't returned. If she had, there'd be a kettle steaming on the hob. As for the teaching staff, they turned up at the last minute with, it often seemed, the boys arriving on their heels. Most of them had rooms in the village, though one or two younger ones slept on the premises in the box-like privacy of specially constructed cubicles at each end of a dormitory.

Having climbed to her room at the top of the house and unpacked her suitcase, Miss Spurling decided it was time to do something about her bicycle. She wished she had thought of asking the driver of the taxi that had brought her to put it on his roof rack and deliver it to Mr Witherspoon, except that he'd been a surly fellow and would almost certainly have grumbled, if not flatly refused.

Returning downstairs she decided to call Mr Witherspoon from the pay phone in the main hall. He had a shop in the village where he repaired everything from lawn mowers to pots and pans, with bicycle tyres included.

'It's Miss Spurling at Warren Hall,' she said when she recognised his voice on the line. 'I have a puncture.'

'But term hasn't started, miss,' he replied with Mad Hatter logic.

'It happened at the end of last term,' she said patiently. 'Can you collect and repair it?'

'Where is it?'

'Here, at the school.'

'Trouble is, my van's off the road. I might be able to pick it up tomorrow,' he said doubtfully. 'I'm right behind with my work, being out yesterday and this morning looking for Joe.'

'Joe?'

'Joe Atherly. He's disappeared. Didn't you know?'

'No, I've only just returned.'

'Oh, well, you wouldn't know then, but we've been looking for him everywhere.'

'What about the police?'

'Oh, they've been helping too.'

Miss Spurling was silent for a moment. Then, unwilling to be deflected from the purpose of her call, she said, 'Well, what about my bicycle, Mr Witherspoon? What time will you collect it tomorrow? It's most inconvenient to be without it.'

'I could come up early.'

'As early as you like.'

'Say eight o'clock. I'll have my van back later today.'

'Eight o'clock will be fine. Come round to the rear of the school and I'll meet you there.'

True to his word, Mr Witherspoon arrived at eight the next morning just as Miss Spurling was emerging from the house.

'Where is it, this bicycle of yours?' he asked with unaccustomed briskness.

'In that shed,' she said, pointing.

They walked in silence toward the structure in question, Miss Spurling purposefully, Mr Witherspoon loping at her side.

'Locked is it?' he enquired as they reached the door.

She shook her head. 'One of the boys managed to break in last term and it hasn't been repaired. At least, I hope it hasn't as I don't have the key.' She was reasonably sure that Mr Thurston would have had weightier things on his mind than the repair of a shed door.

'Hope your bicycle hasn't been nicked,' Mr Witherspoon remarked with a touch of malice.

Miss Spurling ignored the gibe. Seizing the rusty knob of the door she gave it a good tug. The door came open and two moths flew out. The interior smelt of dust and linseed oil. Stepping inside she took hold of a corner of the tarpaulin and pushed it back.

'There it is. I'm afraid it needs a good dust.'

'No time to worry about that now,' Mr Witherspoon observed. 'I'll get the lad to wipe it over.' Mr Witherspoon's lad was all of thirty years old, but was never referred to as anything else.

Mr Witherspoon took hold of the bicycle with both hands and

dragged it out of the shed. 'Looks to me as if you may need a new inner tube.'

'But that one's almost new.'

'Not now it isn't. You've ripped it badly.' Glancing about him, he added, 'Could do with a shed like this myself.' Then: 'That's a useful-looking tool. Wonder if Mr Thurston wants to get rid of it?'

To Miss Spurling the tool in question would not have looked amiss in one of the Tate Gallery's exhibitions of modern sculpture. Leaving her to hold the bicycle he clambered over a mound of cricket netting to reach for the object that had taken his fancy. Suddenly he paused and stared into one of the further recesses of the shed.

'There's a body in here,' he said hoarsely.

'What are you talking about?' Miss Spurling asked impatiently.

'I'm blessed if it isn't Joe Atherly. I recognise his shirt.' He turned round uneasily on top of the netting and met Miss Spurling's querulous gaze. 'He's dead.'

After a moment's hesitation she clambered up to join him astride the pile of netting.

Joe Atherly lay in an untidy heap as if he had been heaved over like a sack of potatoes.

Except that sacks of potatoes weren't usually covered in blood. 'You'd better get back and open your shop,' Miss Spurling said in a voice used to giving orders. 'And take my bicycle with you. I still need it repaired. Meanwhile, I'll telephone the police.'

A stubborn expression came over Mr Witherspoon's face. 'I'll come with you,' he said. 'It was me who found Joe's body.'

'We can't both talk on the phone,' Miss Spurling remarked tartly. 'Much better that I should do so while you return to the village. You needn't worry that I won't give credit where credit is due.'

'You'll tell them it was me who found Joe?'

'Certainly, I will.'

'I still think I ought to be with you when you phone,' he said. 'They'll want to interview me when they know I found the body.'

'Of course they will, but not on the phone. They'll either come to your shop or get you to go to the police station.'

Mr Witherspoon considered this for a few moments and seemed won over.

'Tell 'em I'll be in the shop,' he said. His expression brightened. 'Wouldn't do no harm if I phoned 'em myself when I get back.'

'That's up to you,' Miss Spurling observed frostily.

He carried her bicycle over to his van and put it in the back, while she hurried indoors.

Though she had not seen Mr Thurston since her return the previous afternoon, she assumed he was in residence. She wondered whether she should inform him of the gruesome discovery before phoning the police or whether to call the police immediately and then seek out the headmaster. In the event she decided to report the matter to the police without delay before Mr Witherspoon could get in with his own garbled version. She was aware that the police would be displeased by all the trampling about inside the shed. Any existing footprints were likely to have been eliminated and though she didn't intend denying Mr Witherspoon his moment of glory, she would make it clear that it was *he* who had been primarily responsible for disturbing the scene. If he was anxious to claim the credit for discovering the body, he could also take everything that went with it.

Using the phone in the main hall, she dialled 999 and asked for the police.

'I wish to report the discovery of a body at Warren Hall School, Greenborough,' she said when the connection was made. 'I have reason to believe it's the body of Mr Joe Atherly . . .'

'Hold on a tick. Did you say you'd found a body?'

'Yes.'

'And you think it's someone called Atherly?'

'Yes.'

'What makes you think that?'

'Mr Witherspoon, who actually discovered it, is sure it's Mr Atherly.'

'And who are you?'

'I'm Miss Spurling, the matron at Warren Hall.'

'Where are you speaking from?'

'The school,' Miss Spurling replied with a touch of impatience. 'It'd be a good thing if you sent some of your officers along immediately rather than ask all these questions.'

'I have to be satisfied it's not a hoax call.'

'I'm not in the habit of making hoax calls to the police.'

'I'm glad to hear it. Stay where you are and someone will be along.'

The line went dead and Miss Spurling replaced the receiver. Almost immediately it started to ring and she grabbed it before Mr Thurston or anyone else could appear on the scene.

'This is the police. Are you the person who's just reported the finding of a body at Warren Hall School?'

'Yes, I am.'

'Right. Just checking. Stay put and don't touch anything.'

Miss Spurling allowed herself a small grim smile. Mr Witherspoon could squirm his way out of that one as best he could. Replacing the receiver again, she made her way up the staircase that led to the headmaster's private quarters and knocked heavily on his door.

'Who's that?' a muffled voice called out.

'It's matron, Mr Thurston.'

A moment later the door opened and the headmaster stood there in his dressing gown. He hadn't shaved and looked half asleep.

'When did you get back?' he asked, almost aggressively.

'Yesterday afternoon. I tried to find you, but you were out. I suppose you know about Joe Atherly being missing?'

'Yes. I helped take part in a search for him.'

'His body's in the shed where you store the cricket nets. Mr Witherspoon and I found it there this morning. He's been murdered by the look of it.'

She was startled by the effect her news had on the headmaster. For a second or two, he looked as if he had been turned into stone, then he leaned unsteadily against the door frame.

'Surely you can't be right,' he said in a croak.

'I'm afraid it's true.'

'Oh, my God! I must have some time to think before we notify the police.'

'I've already phoned them.'

He glared at her furiously. 'How dare you without first speaking to me!'

Miss Spurling was never easily cowed. 'I wasn't even sure you were here,' she remarked calmly. 'In any event, I regard reporting a murder as taking precedence over everything else and I'm sure the police would agree.' She paused. 'May I suggest, Mr Thurston, that you get dressed? They'll be arriving shortly.'

Making a succession of inarticulate noises which seemed to reflect both fear and anguish, he disappeared back into his flat, leaving Miss Spurling to return downstairs. Five minutes later, while she was standing by the front door, he came hurrying down. He had put on a black polo neck sweater and a pair of dark green corduroy slacks. He also appeared to have shaved rather hurriedly.

'Do you mean the shed with the broken lock?' he asked in an agitated voice as he prepared to dash out of the building.

'Yes, but . . .'

'I must see for myself before the police come. Keep them talking till I get back.'

Miss Spurling clutched at his arm. 'They were most insistent that the scene shouldn't be disturbed, Mr Thurston. I really don't think you should . . .'

He tugged his arm free and giving her a furious look disappeared down the corridor leading to the side entrance. Miss Spurling, meanwhile, began to unlock the fortress-like front door. She had just got it open when she saw a police car coming up the drive in a cloud of dust. It lurched to a halt and a uniformed officer jumped out.

'Are you the person who reported finding a dead body?' he asked sharply.

'Yes.'

'Where is it?'

'In a shed round at the back. I'll show you the way.'

There was no sign of Mr Thurston's return, but she felt under no obligation to protect him from his own rash behaviour.

They had just rounded the last corner of the building and she was pointing at the shed whose door was open and swinging slightly in the breeze when the headmaster emerged.

'Who the hell's that?' the officer asked.

'Mr Thurston. He's the headmaster.'

'Don't you know not to disturb clues at the scene of a crime?' the officer said as they came face to face.

'I'm the . . .'

'I know who you are, sir,' the officer broke in, as he pushed past Thurston and peered inside the shed.

109

'I did ask you to hold the police off until I came back,' the headmaster said to Miss Spurling in a reproachful tone.

She gave him a withering look in return.

'Looks like a herd of buffalo have been having a party in there,' the officer remarked as he rejoined them. 'Whoever it is, he's dead all right. His head's been bashed in. You say it's Mr Atherly, who's been missing for a few days?'

'I didn't go close enough to make an identification,' the headmaster said stiffly.

'Mr Witherspoon recognised Mr Atherly's shirt,' Miss Spurling remarked.

'Who's Mr Witherspoon?'

In commendably few words, she explained how she and Mr Witherspoon had come to visit the shed, while the officer listened with an expression of frowning impatience.

'Right,' he said when she finished. 'I'll call up headquarters from the car. Meanwhile, nobody, and I mean *nobody*, is to enter that shed. Understood?'

Headmaster and matron both nodded obediently.

'This is absolutely terrible,' Thurston said after the officer had gone.

'I agree it's most unfortunate,' Miss Spurling said.

'*Unfortunate*! It's disastrous. The boys'll be back in a few days. Next term's work is bound to suffer. There'll be total disruption.'

'It may not be as bad as you think. The police are not going to leave the body lying there and I imagine their examination of the shed will be completed within forty-eight hours at the outside.'

'And you seriously believe that everything will then return to normal?' he enquired scathingly.

Stung by his rudeness, Miss Spurling said, 'How soon things return to normal will largely depend on yourself, Mr Thurston. You're the headmaster and you set the tone.' In a more reflective voice she went on, 'What I would like to know is what Joe Atherly was doing here in the first place. The inference is that he was meeting somebody. Who?'

Leaving the question unanswered, Bruce Thurston turned and stalked away.

20

During the next couple of hours cars came and went as if Warren Hall School was a checkpoint in a rally. Among the callers was Chief Inspector Stanwick.

Detective Sergeant Travis, who had been the first CID officer on the scene, stepped forward.

'The doctor reckons he's been dead two or three days,' he said. 'It's lucky the weather's been on the cold side or he'd be a bit high by now.'

'Which doctor was that?'

'Dr Angel from the village.'

'I don't want him moved until the pathologist has examined him in situ. Dr Gorringe is on his way now.'

Stanwick had been taught that a good detective absorbed the scene of the crime through his senses, visual, aural and, most important, his sense of smell. Thus for some time he had stood perfectly still inside the shed while he put his senses to work as if they were a team of bloodhounds. As he stared down at the shrunken remnant that had once been a human being, he recalled that it had been Joe Atherly who had discovered the earlier body. It might be no more than a coincidence, but it was worth bearing in mind.

Accompanied by Sergeant Travis he went in search of Bruce Thurston and Miss Spurling and found them sitting in stony silence in the staff dining room.

'I told them to wait here until you came and not go wandering off,' Travis said.

'I resent being made a prisoner in my own home,' Thurston said indignantly.

'Don't feel you're that, Mr Thurston. I'm grateful to you for being on hand. Perhaps you'd tell me what you know about Atherly's death?'

'I suggest you ask Miss Spurling first. She discovered the body.'

'Well, Miss Spurling?'

The matron proceeded to give a now word-perfect account, not omitting to accord Mr Witherspoon as prominent a role as he would have wished.

'I gather,' Stanwick said, 'that Mr Witherspoon has already phoned us, but the officer to whom he spoke had a bit of difficulty understanding his story. You've made it admirably clear, Miss Spurling. It's a pity he went climbing all over the place inside the shed. That won't have helped.' Miss Spurling nodded. Turning to the headmaster, he went on, 'What time did you get back from Wales on Sunday?'

'Around two o'clock. The police phoned me about the break-in at the school and I returned immediately.'

'I understand it was Atherly who reported you had an intruder. Did you speak to him when you got back?'

'Why should I have spoken to him?'

'Did you?'

'I had no reason to do so.'

'Have you any idea what brought him here on . . . well, probably Sunday evening?'

'None at all. I could hardly believe my ears when Miss Spurling said his body was in the store shed.'

'Would he have known you were back?'

The headmaster shook his head violently in response.

'Perhaps he saw me driving through the village on my return,' he said.

'Perhaps. Anyway, you never saw him later that Sunday?'

'Definitely not.'

'Nor had any arrangement to meet him?'

'No, nothing like that at all,' Thurston said, avoiding Stanwick's gaze.

Stanwick rose from his chair. 'I'll obviously want to talk to you both again when I've found out a bit more. Task number one is to find out what Atherly was doing here when he met his death.'

Miss Spurling nodded keenly, but Bruce Thurston remained unnaturally still.

By the end of the day Stanwick knew the cause of Joe Atherly's death and the precise place where he had died. According to Dr Gorringe, he had been felled by a number of frenzied blows to the head which had fractured his skull in several places. The pathologist gave it as his opinion that the blows had continued after Joe was lying unconscious on the ground.

'His murderer was obviously determined that he shouldn't be brought back to life again,' Dr Gorringe said. 'He suffered an assault of great ferocity.'

The scene of the murder turned out to be an open space at the rear of the shed in which his body was found. The shed itself was one of three which stood in a row with about four feet between each. Behind them lay a stretch of rough ground overgrown by coarse grass and weeds, which was some ten feet wide. The rear of the sheds bounded one side while its further limit was a decaying wooden fence beyond which lay the vegetable garden.

It had not been difficult to reconstruct what had happened. Joe had been killed at the rear of the shed and his body dragged round to the front before being hauled inside and dumped behind the pile of netting. Track marks and a trail of bloodstains made this apparent. The weapon had been a long metal peg used for anchoring the cricket nets. After being put to its murderous use, it had been pushed beneath the shed which was raised several inches above ground level.

Stanwick thought it probable that the murderer had arrived in advance of his victim. Having armed himself, he had waited. As he gazed about him, he noticed there were other similar pegs lying in the grass, for the most part old and rust-coated. The whole area, in fact, was a dump for discarded items. There were two empty paint cans, a number of broken cricket stumps and a fractured goal post.

Presumably either Joe or his murderer had suggested meeting there. It was doubly secluded with the boys away on holiday. From what he had learnt so far, Stanwick was certain that Joe had met his death some time on Sunday evening. That meant he would need to question various people about their movements that evening. The sub-postmaster of Greenborough for one. With so much blood at the scene, the murderer could hardly have avoided getting some on his clothing.

It was with these thoughts circulating in his head that he had left the scene of the crime and had gone to call on Mrs Atherly.

As his car turned along the track that led to her cottage and two others, he observed a car parked outside the Atherly home. Aware that news of her husband's death had already been broken

113

to Gwen Atherly, he assumed it belonged to someone conveying their condolences.

He knocked on the front door, which was opened to reveal Lady Cuckfield.

'I was just about to leave, Chief Inspector,' she said. 'Do come in if you want. Poor Gwen! She's bearing up very courageously.' She led the way into the parlour-cum-kitchen. 'It's Chief Inspector Stanwick to see you, Gwen, so I'll leave.' She took one of Mrs Atherly's hands and gave it a fond squeeze. 'Don't forget, if there's anything I can do to help, you have only to ask.'

Gwen Atherly nodded. 'Thank you for coming, dear,' she said.

Stanwick knew that Lady Cuckfield was popular in the village, but was still surprised by the obvious rapport between the two women.

'I'll see myself out,' Lady Cuckfield said, and melted away.

Gwen Atherly was sitting in a high-back chair with a large cushion behind her and two elbow crutches within reach. She was a tall, thin woman with iron-grey hair cut short in an old-fashioned bob and parted in the middle.

Stanwick sat down and spoke awkwardly. 'Please accept my deepest sympathy in the loss of your husband, Mrs Atherly. Do you feel up to answering a few questions?'

'Yes, I'm all right,' she said in a composed voice. 'The worst part was not knowing what had happened to Joe. Now I know, I can come to terms with his death.'

It struck Stanwick as a somewhat cold-blooded attitude, but perhaps sentiment had never played a strong part in their married life.

'When did you last see your husband?' he asked.

'Sunday afternoon between three and four. He went out around then and never came back.'

'When would you have expected him to return?'

'About six o'clock for his tea. And then he'd have been off down to the pub for the evening.'

'Have you any idea where he was going?'

'No. He'd been on the phone quite a bit, but I don't know who he was talking to. The phone's in the front room, but we always sit in here. It's cosier.'

'Did you overhear any of his conversations?'

114

'I did hear him say he'd call round about ten o'clock, but he could have been talking to anyone for all I know.'

'Can you recollect anything else he said? It could be vitally important, Mrs Atherly.'

She frowned. 'I was dozing off while he was talking . . .'

'But you did hear something?' Stanwick said eagerly.

'I do remember the conversation ending with Joe saying, "See you at ten." '

'That's very helpful,' Stanwick said encouragingly. 'Any other bit you can recall?'

'I remember hearing the word "school".'

'Might Joe have been saying he'd meet the person at the school?'

'I suppose it could have been that.'

'Have you any idea where Joe was between leaving home and meeting someone at ten o'clock that evening?' She shook her head and Stanwick went on, 'Had Joe expressed any fears for his life recently?'

'No,' she said, clearly surprised by the question.

'Had his pattern of behaviour altered at all since he discovered Harry Wells' body?'

'Pattern of behaviour?' she repeated as if he had suddenly broken into Chinese.

'Had he been behaving differently?'

'He sometimes talked as if he'd won the pools when all he'd done was back an evens favourite,' she said with an unmistakable note of scorn.

'Did he flash money around?'

'Not in front of me. It was just so much talk, if you want my opinion.' She paused. 'Not that he used to tell me everything,' she added crossly.

'You know that it was as a result of his action that Mr Pickard was arrested on the school premises and charged with burglary?'

'Yes.'

'Did Joe talk about it?'

'Just said he'd helped the police,' she said in a scathing tone. 'He liked to talk big.'

'What was he doing near the school when he saw the light that aroused suspicions?'

'No idea. Joe didn't like being asked questions about what he was up to. Sometimes he'd tell me things, but if he didn't . . .' She gave a shrug.

'How long had you been married?'

'Over fifty years.'

'So you've celebrated your golden wedding?'

'Don't know that it was anything to celebrate,' she said in a tired voice.

Stanwick reckoned it was a comment that probably summed up her married life. He had lived long enough to know that not every couple who had reached their seventies were an automatic Darby and Joan.

He was on the verge of departure when he paused by the door and said, 'I suppose you've known Sir Denzil and Lady Cuckfield a long time?'

She looked at him suspiciously. 'Sir Denzil was a boy at Warren Hall when my father was the groundsman,' she said after a pause.

'That was when Joe first began working there?'

'Yes.'

'Where did Lady Cuckfield's family come from? They weren't local, were they?'

'As far as I know they lived up Derbyshire way. That was where she and Sir Denzil got married. Of course he was just plain Mr Denzil in those days. They moved into Greenborough Court after his parents' death. Must have been well over thirty years ago. When shall I be able to bury Joe?' she asked abruptly.

'As soon as the coroner releases the body, which shouldn't be too long.'

It affronted his sense of dignity when the bodies of murder victims sometimes had to spend weeks, and even longer, in refrigerated drawers awaiting burial. He accepted the necessity on occasions, but still found it repugnant.

He reckoned in the present case that 'forensic' was his best hope and prayed that the team of officers combing the scene with the determination of a colony of ants would find something which would cause the laboratory to let out a cry of 'eureka'.

Bidding Gwen Atherly goodbye, he returned to his car, watched with interest by her neighbours. He decided to make a further visit before returning to the scene of the crime. Adrian Pickard was still firmly in his sights and the time had come to question him further.

116

As he walked across the sward of grass that separated the post office cottage from the road, he was able to see through to the garden at the rear. A figure was bending over a bonfire at the far end and as it straightened up he could see it was Pickard.

He took the path that led round the side of the cottage and was weaving his way through a clutch of fruit trees before Adrian Pickard swung round and saw him. He had a garden fork in his hands and thrust it into the ground as Stanwick approached.

'Got a bonfire going, I see,' Stanwick observed civilly. 'May I enquire what you're burning?'

'Usual garden rubbish. Here, take the fork and rake it over to satisfy yourself I'm not burning any clothing.'

'What makes you say that?'

'Because isn't that what you suspect? That I'm destroying bloodstained clothing?'

For a few moments the two men stared at one another with hostility. Then Stanwick took the fork and began sifting. By the time he had finished, his eyes were smarting from the smoke and he knew there were no items of clothing in the smouldering pile.

'I'm afraid I've not done your bonfire much good,' he said.

'That doesn't matter as long as you're satisfied.'

'You accused me of looking for bloodstained clothing. Why bloodstained?'

Pickard looked taken aback. 'Because . . . er. . . murder involves spilt blood.'

'Not necessarily. A murderer who strangles someone wouldn't normally be spattered with his victim's blood. Nor one who used a firearm at a range of several yards.'

'I see what you mean,' Adrian said uncomfortably. 'It's just that the layman associates murder with blood.'

'Or was it because you knew Joe Atherly had had his head beaten in? And if so, how did you know?'

'I heard this morning from Mrs Ives, who helps out in the post office, that Joe Atherly's body had been found. She had called in at Mr Witherspoon's shop and he was telling everybody how he had found it in one of the school sheds.'

'Was he also promulgating the cause of death?'

'He said there was a lot of dried blood all over the place. I assumed from that the murderer must have got some on himself. It stands to reason, doesn't it?'

Stanwick felt like an angler who hooks a fat trout, only to see it give a couple of wriggles and drop back into the water. He was determined, however, that this particular trout should not become aware of his chagrin.

'Can you tell me where you spent last Sunday evening?' he asked in his most official voice.

'I took my wife for a drive in the afternoon and we got home around four thirty. I then made tea and we watched television for a bit. My wife hadn't been feeling very well all day and decided to go up to bed soon after seven. I took her up a cup of Bovril and some dry toast and half an hour later when I went to collect the tray, she was asleep. I spent the evening watching the telly and ploughing my way through the Sunday papers.'

'Did you go out at all?'

'Only for a breath of fresh air around nine o'clock. I didn't stay out more than fifteen minutes.'

'Where did you go?' Stanwick asked.

'Only as far as the entrance to Greenborough Court and back home again.'

'Meet anyone while you were out?'

'Not a soul.'

'What were you wearing?'

'Let me think. An old pair of jeans and an even older sweater. A navy blue one if you want to know.'

'May I see them?'

'Certainly.'

His alacrity warned Stanwick that an inspection of the garments was unlikely to bring him any joy.

'I'll fetch them,' he said, walking toward the cottage. A couple of minutes later he reappeared holding a pair of jeans and a chunky blue sweater. 'Here you are, Chief Inspector. They may not be exactly clean, but at least they're not bloodstained.'

It was a bit later when the two men were still standing in the garden that Margaret emerged through a door that led out of the kitchen. She was holding a plastic bucket of clothes and gave her husband a small wave.

'Bring your friend in for a drink,' she called out. 'I'm just going to hang these things out to dry. I see you put your jeans into the machine for a second wash. Heaven knows what you got on them.'

Stanwick moved quickly toward her. 'I'm Detective Chief Inspector Stanwick, madam, and I'm taking possession of those jeans.' He stared into the plastic bucket which lay on the ground between them. 'And possibly other items as well.' He turned back to Adrian who was standing as though mesmerised by what he was witnessing. 'I don't think I need retain the pair of jeans you handed me. Nor the blue sweater; particularly as I see there's a red one that's just been washed. I'll have that, instead.'

21

'The wretched man has taken away practically all Adrian's clothes,' Margaret exclaimed with considerable indignation when she called Rosa shortly after Stanwick's departure. 'It's disgraceful. Surely the police have no right to behave in such a high-handed manner.'

Her sense of outrage positively sizzled down the line, enhanced, Rosa couldn't help feeling, by the recognition that she herself was in part responsible for what had happened.

'You say that Joe Atherly's body was discovered this morning?' Rosa put in when she had an opportunity.

'Yes. They think he'd been dead since Sunday evening. It was found by the school matron when she went to get her bicycle . . .' Rosa heard muffled voices, then Margaret said, 'Adrian says it was actually found by a Mr Witherspoon, who has a repair shop in the village. Anyway, what's it matter who found it? The point is what do you suggest we do?'

'Perhaps I could have a word with Adrian?' Rosa said in a quiet, placating tone.

'All right. But something's got to be done. If they take any more of his clothes, he'll have to go about wrapped in a blanket. It would serve them right if he marched up and down outside the police station without any clothes at all. Here's Adrian now . . .'

'Sorry about that, Rosa,' Adrian said in an apologetic voice. 'But Margaret's furious with the police.'

'So I gathered. Can we speak freely?'

'Yes. She's gone upstairs.'

'Does she know about the burglary charge?'

'No. I keep putting off telling her.'

'I suggest sooner rather than later.'

'Yes, I will.'

'Because,' Rosa went on, 'if the police suspect you of killing Joe Atherly, I think we'd better tell them straightaway what you were doing at the school that evening. I'd prefer not to divulge your defence before you appear in court, but our hand may be forced by events.'

'I understand,' he said meekly.

'What was all that about the garments which the police took away having been given a second wash?' Rosa asked.

Adrian sighed. 'It was all most unfortunate. Margaret doesn't normally touch the washing machine. She pretends not to understand it. I had emptied it and was going to deal with the clothes later, but I got immersed in my bonfire and then Chief Inspector Stanwick arrived. Margaret found the basket of damp things in the kitchen and decided to play the domesticated housewife, a role that doesn't suit her anyway. She may have wanted an excuse to come into the garden and see who I was talking to. Whatever the reason, her entry on the scene couldn't have been less timely.'

Rosa was taken aback by the bitterness of his tone, but attributed it to the stress he had been under.

'That still doesn't answer my question,' she said. 'Why did the jeans and the red sweater require a further wash?'

'Because there was blood on them . . . Not human blood. A dog's blood. I ran over a dog on my way home on Sunday evening. It suddenly dashed across the road and I couldn't avoid it. I stopped and got out of the car and could see it was dead. I picked it up and threw it into a ditch . . .'

'Do you know whose dog it was?' Rosa broke in.

'It was a mongrel and belonged to one of the gypsy families who are encamped in that area. They all have dogs which roam almost wild. I know you're supposed to report hitting a dog to the police, but I didn't try and find the owner because they're a rough bunch and can turn nasty with very little provocation. And the last thing I wanted was trouble. It was around eleven o'clock and not the hour to go knocking on caravan doors.' He paused. 'Also I felt I was in enough trouble without adding to it. When I got home I examined my clothing and found I had some of the animal's blood on my jeans and the red sweater I'd been wearing. I would have put them immediately into the washing machine, but I knew it was on the blink – in fact it wasn't repaired until Monday afternoon – so I locked them in the boot of my car and left them there until Monday evening when they had their first wash. Then this morning I decided to give them another go.'

'And you've not told Margaret that you ran over this dog?'

'No, it would only worry her.'

'But you could have told the police, couldn't you?'

'Look, Rosa, you know how it is, the moment to do or say something passes and can't be recaptured. I'd already deceived Stanwick by handing him clothes I'd not been wearing on Sunday evening. Moreover, I'd told him I had only gone out for a brief walk, which wasn't true. A few white lies seemed the best option.'

Rosa recalled somebody once saying that lies were apt to have short legs. Adrian's looked like having none at all.

'Where did you drive to on Sunday evening?' she asked.

'To a village where I wasn't known. I just went out for a quiet drink.'

'What was the name of the village?'

'Nabb Cross. I had a drink at the Golden Hind there.'

'So you were out around the time Joe Atherly is supposed to have met his death? Presumably Margaret knew you were out?'

'She went to bed early as she hadn't been feeling well all day. She took a couple of sleeping pills and went out like a light. I told the chief inspector that.'

'But you also told him you spent the evening at home apart from a fifteen-minute walk?'

'It seemed the easier option.'

Rosa sighed. 'You're in a mess, Adrian. How big a mess remains to be seen. Next time Stanwick wishes to interview you, tell him you insist on having your solicitor present.'

'I wanted to tell him that this morning, but I never had the chance. There I was starting a bonfire when he appeared in the garden and took me completely by surprise.'

'Don't get taken by surprise again,' Rosa said drily. 'And, Adrian, don't tell any more lies. Not to the police, not to anybody. Remember that white lies, in particular, can assume a somewhat different hue later on.'

22

For most of her life Rosa had avoided taking any part in politics. Like most people she felt free to criticise, but had no desire to play an active role. She regretted that a democratic system had so many unattractive features, but supposed you couldn't have the one without a helping of the other.

The last thing she ever dreamt of doing was attending political meetings. But on the evening of the day that Adrian Pickard had sunk deeper into trouble, she had promised to lend her support to an old girl friend who was standing for election to her local borough council. Rosa couldn't think why anyone, including Annabel Farthing, should want to become a councillor and said as much to her friend.

'They're such a ghastly lot,' Annabel had said, 'that I feel I must stop being an armchair critic and take action.'

'Are you really expecting to be able to change things?'

'No, but I must try. Anyway, Rosa, do come to this meeting and give me your moral support.'

'I'll come and listen to you, but don't expect me to hang about afterwards.'

'Oh, you must stay and meet the star of the evening. A real live member of the government is coming to speak. His name's Martin Cuckfield, but I don't suppose you've ever heard of him. He's only a junior minister,' she added with a note of apology.

'I've not only heard of him, I've met him.'

'Then you must come, Rosa. Promise.'

And Rosa had promised.

The meeting was scheduled to begin at eight and she arrived in good time. There were already about forty to fifty people in the hall. A tousle-haired young man was at the door, eyeing arrivals. He was wearing a badge which read 'Vote for Farthing' and he gave Rosa a cheerful smile.

'Sit where you like,' he said. 'Didn't I see you at last week's meeting at the school?'

Rosa shook her head. 'No, I don't live in this area, but Annabel is an old friend.'

'Great! Nice to meet you . . .'

'Rosa Epton.'

'Of course.'

'Why of course?' Rosa enquired in surprise.

'Annabel's mentioned you. You're a solicitor, yes?'

'Yes.'

'By the way I'm Tim Offord. I've got to hang around here for when the minister arrives. It's been nice meeting you, Rosa.'

Rosa moved into the body of the hall and sat down at the end of a row so that she could make an easy escape if necessary. Annabel was on the platform engaged in earnest conversation with a red-bearded man and a woman who looked as if she had just emerged from a wind-tunnel. Not only her hair, but her clothes as well gave the impression of having been assaulted by a force nine gale.

'Should be an interesting evening,' said a voice at her side.

She turned her head to find that the speaker was a small, neat man of indeterminate age. Rosa decided he was probably a minor civil servant or an accounts clerk in some large organisation. He either lived with an elderly mother or alone in house-proud anonymity. She was juggling with these alternatives when he spoke again.

'I've really come to hear Mr Cuckfield. He's said to be one of the most promising junior members of the government. He could even be a future prime minister.' In a confiding tone he went on, 'It's not often I can get out of an evening as my wife has an evening job, and with four children under the age of ten one of us is tied to the house. But she's not working this evening and her sister's gone round to keep her company.'

Rosa accepted this stream of information with a series of nods and smiles.

'Will you be voting for Annabel Farthing?' she asked.

'I expect so, but I'm your floating voter. It's up to her. She's got to win my vote. What about you?'

'I've only come because she's an old friend. I don't live in the borough.'

'Oh, I see. Nice person, is she?'

'Delightful.'

'You think she'll make a good councillor, if elected?'

'I'm sure of it. She'll be extremely conscientious.'

'Then I'll vote for her.'

At that moment the man with the red beard called for silence and made a few introductory remarks. As he was preparing to sit down, Martin Cuckfield arrived on the platform and a lot of hand-shaking ensued, after which Annabel got up and made what Rosa regarded as a thoroughly sensible speech. She hoped it wasn't too sensible. It lacked rhetorical flourishes and was devoid of platitudes. It was greeted with moderate applause. There followed questions from the floor which she fielded like a real pro – or so Rosa thought.

Then it was Martin Cuckfield's turn. After a long-winded introduction the chairman gave him the floor and he launched into a speech which sounded as if it had been delivered many times before. He extolled his party's record in local government and went on to say how important it was that everyone turned out on polling day and voted for Annabel.

To Rosa he gave the impression of being tired and distracted, with his mind a long way from the hall in which he was speaking. Not even a heckler who punctuated the speech with derisive shouts of 'rubbish' produced a reaction. Even allowing that politicians could have off-days like opera singers and tennis players, it was a lack-lustre, rambling performance and Rosa could only hope it wouldn't harm Annabel's chances of election.

As if reading her thoughts, her neighbour said, 'I don't know how he got to be a minister. I've heard better speeches in school debating societies. I'm a teacher,' he added, completing Rosa's disillusionment about his background.

'I agree,' she said, 'but don't let it put you off voting for Annabel.'

'I'd have been better off staying at home and talking to my sister-in-law.'

The speech had clearly had a dampening effect on proceedings for there were few questions and even the hecklers seemed to have become dispirited.

One or two people moved toward the platform and engaged Annabel and red-beard in discussion. But when Rosa looked for Martin Cuckfield he had disappeared.

'Well, I'm off home,' her neighbour said. 'A very disappointing evening. Cuckfield must have got his reputation from somewhere, but I'm afraid he hasn't proved much of an asset to your friend. A vote loser rather than a vote catcher, I'd say.'

With his departure Rosa sat back and waited for those around the platform to disperse. After five minutes or so, only Annabel and red-beard, plus a number of party workers, were left and she made her way up to the front.

'Rosa, darling,' Annabel called out as she approached. 'I couldn't see you anywhere. Were you right at the back?'

'I was sitting behind one of your more massive supporters. I thought your speech was splendid. I wish I could say the same for Martin Cuckfield's.'

Annabel grimaced. 'I think the poor man must have been unwell. He was so nervous, it wasn't true.' With a mischievous smile she added, 'He seemed to become more nervous when I told him you were here.'

'What exactly did you tell him?'

'That an old friend named Rosa Epton had come specially to hear him and was looking forward to meeting him again afterwards. I said I understood you had met at a fête in Greenborough a few weeks ago.'

'And?'

'He muttered that unfortunately he'd have to leave as soon as he'd made his speech.'

'Did he seem to recognise my name?'

'Oh, yes, but I wasn't being serious when I said my mention of you seemed to make him more nervous. It was just that he was in a jittery state.'

Rosa saw that red-beard was waiting to claim Annabel's attention, so made her farewells and turned to go.

'We must definitely meet and have a long talk once the election's over. Remember to give my love to Philip.'

'Peter?'

'Yes, Peter.'

Rosa drove home in a pensive mood. Though it had not been an enjoyable evening, Martin Cuckfield's appearance and behaviour had aroused her curiosity. He had obviously not wanted to see her again, but she could only speculate as to the reason.

23

The next day Rosa was in court in the morning, but had no further engagements. Things were relatively slack in the office, which didn't mean her work had dried up, only that she could afford the luxury of deciding what to do, rather than having her life dictated by circumstances.

It was thus that she set off for Greenborough about three o'clock in the afternoon. She had not let the Pickards know she was coming and didn't, in fact, intend calling on them. Warren Hall School was her destination, though Bruce Thurston was equally unaware of her impending visit. She reckoned, however, that with a new term starting in a few days, she stood a good chance of finding him at home.

She pulled up on the rough gravel drive in front of the house and got out. It was the first time she had seen the school at close quarters. It was one of those enormous nineteenth-century mansions which had been put to institutional use after it ceased to be a private home. Bits had been added down the years and she thought it likely that the interior had been carved up in an effort to adapt it for school use.

The solid outer door was open and through the glass-panelled inner door Rosa could see someone up a step ladder. He appeared to be hanging a picture. She knocked on the door and the man glanced round. Then descending the ladder he came to the door and opened it.

'Can I help you?' he enquired politely.

He was wearing an old-fashioned green baize apron and looked every inch the faithful old retainer.

'I'd like to see Mr Thurston,' Rosa said.

'Is he expecting you, madam?'

'No. Is he in?'

'He's somewhere about. If you wait here, I'll see if I can find him. Who shall I say wants him?'

'Rosa Epton. He may or may not know my name.'

'Are you a prospective parent?'

126

'Not yet,' Rosa replied with a smile.

The man cast her a suspicious look before turning and setting off along a passage. He returned sooner than Rosa expected.

'He's just coming,' he said and climbed back up the step ladder.

A door slammed in the distance and a few seconds later Bruce Thurston appeared.

'Miss Epton, is it? I know your name, but for the moment I can't place you.'

'I'm a solicitor and I'm making a few enquiries on behalf of a client.'

He frowned. 'Am I supposed to know who your client is?'

'Adrian Pickard.'

His jaw dropped and he stared at her with a mixture of emotions in which curiosity and suspicion fought for first place.

'You'd better come along to my study,' he said, curiosity winning by a short head. When they were seated he went on, 'I'm not sure that I should be talking to you in view of the fact that your client is charged with breaking into my school.'

'I don't think you'll feel compromised by anything I say.'

'Are you at liberty to tell me why he broke in? He doesn't appear to have stolen anything and I gather the police are as mystified as I am. Of course since then there's been this ghastly murder and one can't help wondering if the two events are linked in some way.'

Rosa decided that the only way of gaining his co-operation was by telling him what Adrian had been up to. This she now did.

'What an extraordinary story!' he said when she had finished. 'Do the police know?'

'Not yet.'

'I imagine if a court believed him, he'd be acquitted.'

'I would certainly expect that.'

Thurston put his hands to his face and groaned. 'As if I didn't have enough trouble without this. Should the press get hold of it, we'll be on every front page. Coupled with Atherly's death, it'll be the finish of my school.' He gave Rosa a despairing look. 'What exactly has brought you here this afternoon?'

'Would you have any record of where Stephen Willett used to spend the school holidays? I know his parents were in India at the time and that was before the age of jet travel, so I assume he stayed somewhere in this country and only saw his mother and father when they came home by ship.'

'Supposing I was able to tell you,' he said in a thoughtful tone, 'what use would you make of the information?'

'I'd try and find out if there are any leads as to what happened to Stephen Willett. I've read all the newspaper reports of Walter Price's trial, but there's no mention of the boy's background apart from his being a pupil at Warren Hall and his parents living abroad. If you are able to help me, it may or may not get me much further, but I feel I must pursue every possible line.'

'Do you believe Pickard's incredible story?'

'For the moment, yes.'

Thurston stroked his chin with a judicial air. 'I don't see why I shouldn't tell you what you want to know,' he said at length. 'It so happens I dug out the information shortly after the death of the man Wells.' He opened a drawer in his desk and pulled out a dog-eared folder. 'His guardian in this country was his grandfather who lived at Bewick Hall, Kenchapel, in Shropshire.' He closed the folder and glanced up. 'Does that answer your question?'

'Yes. Thank you for telling me. Do you know who lives there now?'

'I've no idea.' He gave her a cheerless smile. 'I'm afraid I can't help you any further.'

'There is one other point,' Rosa said. 'Would it be possible some time between now and my client's court appearance to bring him along to study the school photographs of the period when his father was here?'

'I expect that could be arranged, subject to certain conditions. I suggest you get in touch with me nearer the time.'

'Thank you, I will. I'm very grateful to you for your help. Incidentally, Adrian Pickard is not aware of my visit to you.'

Rosa realised she had taken a risk in telling Thurston as much as she had. She was undoubtedly guilty of a breach of professional confidence, but it was a case where she hoped the end would justify the means.

Of course, should Bruce Thurston ever be charged with Joe Atherly's murder she might find herself in an extremely awkward situation. And that could be understating it.

Impetuosity and lawyer's caution were uneasy bed-fellows, but it was on those occasions that Rosa relied on instinct. And

128

instinct had told her to ignore the dangers and to seek Bruce Thurston's help.

Peter reacted eagerly when Rosa suggested they should drive up to Shropshire at the weekend.

'Kenchapel is about fifteen miles from Shrewsbury, over toward the Welsh border,' she said. 'If we went on Friday evening, we could stay the night in Shrewsbury, pursue our enquiries on Saturday and come home on Sunday.'

'The car needs a bit of exercise,' he said. 'A long journey clears its tubes.'

Rosa didn't consider that a car as expensive as his should have tubes that needed clearing, but decided not to say so.

They arrived in Shrewsbury around eight o'clock and booked in at their hotel, before going in search of a restaurant recommended by Peter's guide-book.

'Let's hope the trip's going to help resolve your doubts about Adrian,' Peter remarked, as they waited for their first course to arrive.

'I hate feeling as uncertain about him as I do,' Rosa said with a sigh. 'Perhaps I'm being unfair and he's merely accident-prone.'

'One thing for sure, he's in trouble up to his neck so that anything you discover which helps to substantiate his story must be to his advantage.'

After an excellent dinner and a good night's rest, not to mention a hearty English breakfast on Peter's part, they set off for Kenchapel shortly before ten o'clock the next morning. Soon they were driving through rolling farmland with distant views of the mid-Welsh hills. The last few miles took them along narrow lanes and then suddenly a sign announced 'Kenchapel welcomes safe drivers'.

'That's us,' Peter said cheerfully. 'Where do you want me to stop?'

'The post office might be a good starting point,' Rosa observed wryly. 'After that we'll look out for the oldest inhabitant.'

They came to some shops where the road broadened and Peter pulled up.

'There's the post office,' he said, pointing at a window of familiar appearance. A blackboard propped against its wall proclaimed that 'pots and toms' were also on sale.

'Pots and toms?' Peter said.

'Potatoes and tomatoes,' Rosa translated for his benefit.

Inside, the small shop was full. There were people buying stamps and sending off parcels at one end, and purchasing chocolate and cigarettes at the other. The air buzzed with conversation and it was apparent that Kenchapel's post office was another gossip mart.

Rosa and Peter joined the stamp queue which led to a bespectacled, grey-haired woman behind a thick glass panel. Presumably, post office employees needed protection even in Kenchapel, though it was difficult to envisage hold-ups in such a peaceful and rustic environment.

When they reached the head of the queue Rosa bought a pound's worth of stamps and, while she was being served, asked the way to Bewick Hall.

'Bewick Hall?' the woman said. 'Do you mean Bewick Hall Estate?'

'Is there no longer a house called Bewick Hall?'

'It was pulled down in the sixties. They built a council estate in the grounds. It's about half a mile on the other side of the village before you get to the furniture factory.' She pointed over her shoulder in a helpful gesture.

'Do you know the name of the people who lived at Bewick Hall before it was pulled down?'

'It'd been empty for years. I think the last owner was an old man named Willett, but that was long before I came here.'

Conscious that the queue behind her was becoming both restive and curious, Rosa thanked the woman and made her way out, followed by Peter.

'The female behind you had ears the size of rhubarb leaves,' he remarked. 'I could see them growing as she tuned in to your conversation.'

While they were standing outside deciding on their next move, the same woman came out. She gave them a quick speculative look and then approached.

'Excuse me,' she said, 'but I couldn't help overhearing your conversation with Emily. You were asking her about Bewick Hall.'

'That's right. I gather it's been pulled down.'

'When I was born, it was still the family home of the Willetts. My father used to help out in the garden there. He'd have been ninety this year and he died only last February.'

130

'Did he ever mention a boy named Stephen Willett who disappeared from his school in the early thirties?'

The woman gave Rosa a knowing look. 'Dad had his own theory about that. He never believed the boy had been murdered.'

'What was his theory?' Rosa asked with immediate interest.

The woman bit her lip as if suddenly overcome by indecision. 'What exactly are you after?'

'I'm a lawyer and I'm making enquiries on behalf of a client. This is a friend, who has driven me here,' she added, indicating Peter.

'You're not from a newspaper?'

'Definitely not.'

'Because I wouldn't want anything I say to be splashed around.'

'I assure you it won't be.'

'Dad wouldn't have liked that.'

'Don't worry.'

'It was always Dad's belief that the boy ran away with a gypsy family. It seems he was a lonely child and there was nobody at the Hall who was anywhere near his own age. According to Dad, he used to spend a lot of time with the Flanagans who lived in a caravan about half a mile away. There was Reuben Flanagan, his wife Bessie and two small kids. It seems that the Willett boy took a considerable shine to Reuben, who taught him various gypsy ways. How to mend things that other people had discarded and how to chop wood without wasting any. That sort of thing.' She paused. 'Gypsies didn't have great cars in those days, though Reuben Flanagan had an old van he used to drive. Dad told me that the boy would take food to the Flanagans, apparently without the cook at the Hall noticing, so he was always welcome.'

'How old would Reuben Flanagan have been?'

'In his late twenties. Bessie was several years younger. According to Dad she was the sort to go on having a baby a year until she lost count. Anyway, the thing is that the Flanagans had upped and left the district at about the same time as the Willett boy disappeared from school and Dad was always sure the two events were connected.'

'Did he ever voice his suspicions to the police?'

She shook her head. 'Dad was always one to keep himself to himself. And as he used to say, he didn't have any proof. I think he was afraid of being snubbed.'

'Supposing,' Rosa said after a thoughtful pause, 'Price had been convicted and had been about to be hanged, do you think your father might then have gone to the police?'

'Why should he have?' she said in a tone that bridled. 'It was still only his opinion and who was he against all the legal bigwigs who thought differently? Dad never tried to force his views down other people's throats. But that didn't mean he wouldn't stick to what he believed.'

'And that was his belief? That Stephen Willett had not been murdered, but had gone off with this gypsy family?'

The woman nodded. 'He never wavered in his view.'

'Did your Dad see Stephen when he was here during the school holidays?'

'Yes. Felt sorry for him, not having anyone of his own age to play with.'

'What sort of boy was he?'

'Quiet. Dad said he was like one of those peat fires that burn away beneath the surface without anything showing above ground.'

'Was your father's view shared by others in the village?'

'I think most of them were inclined to believe that the boy had been murdered and that it was merely a coincidence the Flanagans left the district about the same time. And, of course, they may have been right. Nobody'll ever know now.'

Rosa gave a thoughtful nod. She didn't feel able to tell the woman that her client's story confirmed her father's belief.

'You've been extraordinarily helpful and I'm most grateful.' With an apologetic smile, she added, 'I don't even know your name.'

'Mrs Nance.'

'I'm Rosa Epton, a solicitor from London. How fortunate you were behind me in the post office queue or we'd never have met.'

'There's a saying in the village that if you want to know anything, ask Mrs Nance,' observed the owner of the name complacently.

After thanking her again, Rosa and Peter walked over to their car.

'Where to now?' Peter asked.

'Let's drive past Bewick Hall Estate. Having come all this way, we might as well have a look, not that it's likely to provide any inspiration.'

'Meeting Mrs Nance was an alternative to inspiration. After that why don't we drive towards those hills and find somewhere to have lunch?'

'Let's do that,' Rosa said.

Five minutes later Bewick Hall Estate came into view on their left. There were about a hundred small houses clustered together, making an eyesore of brick and mortar in the green countryside.

'You can't even tell where the original house was,' Peter remarked as they drove past.

'It's as if they wanted to obliterate all traces of the Willett family,' Rosa added.

'Are you now satisfied that Adrian must be Stephen Willett's son?' Peter asked when they had driven some distance in silence.

She nodded. 'I think what Mrs Nance told us clinches it. Stephen wasn't murdered and Adrian's account of his father's background, even allowing for all the gaps, is too fantastic to be an invention.' A note of nagging doubt was back in her voice when she spoke again. 'But if Adrian *is* a Willett and even if he's told me the truth as to why he broke into the school, does it necessarily follow that he had nothing to do with either of the two recent deaths?'

'It doesn't follow at all,' Peter said bleakly.

'You don't like him, do you?'

'As a matter of fact, the only time we met, I did quite like him. I found him friendly and easy to talk to. It's what has happened since then.'

'You don't think Margaret's in any danger, do you?'

'No. Atherly's and Wells' deaths have links with the past. Your godmother has no such links.'

'But if Adrian is already a double murderer, would he hesitate to kill again if he felt himself threatened?'

'I can't think of anything more likely to threaten him than the sudden death of his wife.'

'But it wouldn't be difficult to make her death look like an accident, Peter. She's old and not too physically fit.'

'It's time you had a drink,' Peter said firmly. 'We'll stop at the next pub we see.'

'You're right,' Rosa replied. 'I mustn't get paranoid about my difficult client.' She paused. 'It's not that he's personally difficult; just that he sticks to me like a burr.'

They spent the afternoon driving through unspoilt countryside over the Welsh border, stopping once to enjoy an hour's walk in clean, fresh air.

'I feel much better for our walk,' Rosa said, as they headed back to Shrewsbury.

'You'll feel even better after a bath, a drink and a good dinner, in that order.'

'Pity we have to go back to London tomorrow.'

'I know. But all the more reason to make the most of this evening.'

'You're off somewhere on Monday, aren't you?'

'Zürich. I'll be back the same day. What about you?'

'I'm planning a visit to St Catherine's House.'

'It sounds vaguely familiar. What goes on there?' Peter asked with a frown.

'It's the office of Population Censuses and Surveys. What used to be called the Registry of Births, Deaths and Marriages.'

Though Peter gave her a look which asked for further enlightenment, none was immediately forthcoming.

24

Detective Chief Inspector Stanwick was itching to make an arrest and charge Adrian Pickard with murder. Detective Sergeant Travis, who had been in the police much longer than Stanwick and who belonged to the old sweat brigade of police officer, was even more eager and was impatient of the constraints recent legislation had placed on police activity.

Having discussed the case with his superior officers, Stanwick sought an interview with the local head of the Crown Prosecution Service in the hope of obtaining his blessing on an early arrest. Accordingly, he and Travis arrived at the CPS's office on Monday afternoon ready to do battle.

Mr Seale, the chief crown prosecutor for the area, received them with the martyred air of someone whose time was spent dodging the slings and arrows of outrageous fortune.

'I've read all the statements you've sent me,' he said, giving Stanwick a mournful look, 'but I'm not too happy about their probative value. I agree there's a wealth of suspicion against this fellow Pickard but does it amount to more than suspicion? Suspicion isn't evidence, therefore five or ten suspicious factors carry no more evidential weight than a single one. In other words, no weight at all.' He smiled lugubriously. 'It doesn't matter how many times you multiply zero, the result can never be other than zero. Do I make myself plain?' Ignoring Sergeant Travis' mutinous sniff, he went on, 'What in your view, Chief Inspector, is the strongest piece of evidence against Pickard?'

'His proven lies. On the Sunday evening when Atherly met his death, Pickard left home and spent time drinking at the Golden Hind in Nabb Cross. He was recognised by someone from Greenborough, who is prepared to give evidence. When I questioned Pickard, he told me he'd been at home the whole evening apart from a short walk which hadn't kept him out for more than fifteen minutes. Why lie about that? Moreover, I'm pretty sure it was he who ran over a dog on the outskirts of Greenborough. It was found in a ditch, but the driver never stopped or attempted to trace the owner. Why not? When I asked him to let me have the clothing he'd been wearing that evening, he produced a pair of jeans and a blue sweater. Then just as I was leaving, his wife came into the garden to hang out some washing, which included a pair of jeans and a red sweater, and commented on their having needed a second wash. The person who recognised him in the Golden Hind is certain he was wearing a red and not a blue sweater. So why did he lie about the clothes he'd been wearing? I suggest there's only one answer to all his lies . . . guilt.'

'Have you received the lab report on his clothing? It could be crucial. So why not wait?'

'They've not yet completed their examination. And I don't want to run the risk of Pickard disappearing.'

'Do we know what time he arrived home that evening?'

Stanwick shook his head. 'His wife had gone to bed early and taken a sleeping pill.'

'Can anyone say what time he left the Golden Hind?'

'Nobody actually saw him leave. He was still there shortly before ten and had departed by ten thirty.'

Seale turned the pages of the interim file Stanwick had sent him. 'I see that Dr Gorringe estimates that death took place between nine o'clock and midnight on Sunday evening,' he observed.

'When Pickard was out and about, despite his lies to the contrary,' Stanwick said.

'What about motive?' the crown prosecutor asked. 'I know we don't have to prove one, but it always helps. Juries like to have a motive in the same way a motorist needs a signpost to find his way.'

'It was Atherly who shopped him.'

'Hardly a motive for murder.'

'I tend to agree. Personally, I think it was much more likely that Atherly was blackmailing Pickard.'

'In respect of what?'

'It could have been something to do with Wells' death. It was Atherly who discovered the body and I've always felt he knew more than he told us.'

'You may be right, but it's only conjecture.'

After a pause, Stanwick said, 'So you don't think we have enough evidence yet to charge him?'

'I'm afraid not.' He stared at the two officers over the top of his spectacles. 'What you need, Chief Inspector, is one solid piece of evidence linking Pickard to the scene of the crime. Find that and we're in business.'

'Nitpicking lawyers,' Sergeant Travis observed sourly as they returned to their car. 'They're so cautious, they drive you mad. If we worked on the same basis, we'd never arrest anyone without first taking out an insurance policy.'

'No point in getting angry. We must sift through everything again and hope to find something we've missed. Detective work is nine parts slogging routine and one part luck.' He paused. 'I must say we could do with a bit of luck.'

Travis let out a grunt that seemed to indicate he had no time for philosophising.

The next morning a team of young officers were detailed to return to Warren Hall School and search for clues which might have been overlooked the first time.

'And I don't care if you take the effing shed apart,' Travis instructed them.

At the same time he himself went off to see Gwen Atherly.

'Sorry to trouble you further,' he said, 'but have you thought of anything fresh? I'm afraid this is how it goes in our job. Knocking on the same doors all over again in the hope that somebody has suddenly remembered something.'

She looked at him with a slightly bemused expression and shook her head.

'You've told us your husband was on the phone that Sunday afternoon and you were sure he was making an arrangement to meet someone.' In fact she had been less certain about everything than Travis made out, but it wasn't a time for sowing doubts in a witness' mind. The very reverse. 'Did Joe keep a diary or jot things down to remind him what he had to do?'

'There was his little book,' she said, with a slight frown.

'Do you know where he kept it?'

'In one of his pockets.'

'Is it still there?'

'Unless one of your lot has taken it.'

'It wasn't in any of the pockets of the clothes he was wearing when he was killed or we'd have found it.'

'His things are hanging in the bedroom cupboard upstairs,' she said, with a motion of her head that Travis took as an invitation to go and look for himself.

Five minutes later he returned downstairs. 'I can't find any little book,' he said. 'What colour is it?'

'Red. It must be up there somewhere unless somebody's taken it.' She pulled herself out of her chair and reached for her crutches.

'Do you want a hand?' Travis asked.

'No, I can manage if you give me time. Now that Joe's gone, I'll probably move my bed downstairs into the front room. It'll make things easier.'

Travis followed her into the bedroom and watched while she rummaged through the pockets of three jackets. One was part of Joe's best suit; another was a brown tweed jacket with patched elbows; the third was a well-worn gamekeeper's jacket with large pockets on either side. Mrs Atherly let out an exclamation as she brought out a small red notebook from the right-hand pocket.

'You didn't look properly,' she said.

'I was sure I felt everywhere.'

'And you a policeman! When we get downstairs you can make me a cup of tea.'

She handed him the notebook which had a short ballpoint pen clipped to its outer cover.

'Looks like a betting shop pen,' Travis remarked sardonically.

'Very likely. Joe used to write down the names of his winners. Not that there were many of those. He'd have needed a book the size of a family bible to record his losers.' Her tone was tart and indicated her disapproval of her late husband's betting activities.

While the kettle was boiling, Travis flicked through the pages.

'One rab,' he read out. 'What does that mean?'

'A rabbit. He used to set snares.'

'And the next day he apparently caught a hare.' He turned another page. 'Would Mr T be Mr Thurston?'

'Could be.'

'Mr T, W.H., 11,' he read out. 'I suppose that could mean meet Mr Thurston at Warren Hall at eleven o'clock?'

'Mr Thurston was always asking Joe to do odd jobs up at the school.'

'Sir D is obviously Sir Denzil. It looks as if Joe had an appointment with him on the Friday before he was killed. Who would Mr P be?'

She shrugged. 'Could be Mr Pickard.'

'Did Joe do business with him?'

'Not as I know. But Joe didn't tell me everything. Not by a long chalk, he didn't.'

'I see that Streamline Sal won at Plumpton on the seventeenth. She was the two-to-one favourite and Joe had a couple of pounds on her.'

'When Joe had a winner, he kept it to himself. I never saw any of the money.' She glanced across at the cooker. 'The kettle's boiling. Put down that book and make the tea.'

The sergeant obediently did so and brought a cup over to where she was sitting. After pouring himself a cup, he again gave his attention to the notebook and turned to the final entry.

'Well, well,' he murmured, 'this is interesting.'

'Found something, have you?' Gwen Atherly enquired, casually.

'Yes. The last entry of all reads, "Sun eve, Mr P, W.H., 10".'
He passed the notebook to her. 'You read it,' he said.

She groped for her spectacles which had slipped down the side of the chair and put them on.

'Presumably he was going to meet Mr Pickard at the school that evening,' she said unemotionally.

'At ten o'clock,' Travis added. 'I'd love to know why.'

'No good asking me. For all I know, he could have met all sorts of people that day.' After a pause, she added, 'Joe had a lot of irons in the fire.'

Travis swallowed his tea and got up.

'Thanks for your help, Mrs Atherly. I'll take this notebook with me.'

Gwen watched him depart. Nothing could bring Joe back to life, but she didn't want his death to destroy other lives as well. She felt strangely detached about what had happened and at the same time suffered spasms of apprehension.

Meanwhile, Sergeant Travis was on the phone to headquarters from his car.

'I've found the link that'll put Master Pickard behind bars,' he said triumphantly when Chief Inspector Stanwick came on the line. 'I'm on my way back now.'

25

Margaret Pickard's normally husky voice was vibrant with anger and anxiety when she called Rosa two mornings later. It was around eight thirty and Rosa was about to leave for work.

'The police have been here and have taken Adrian away,' she said. 'They're going to charge him with murder. They must be mad. I don't know what they think they're doing. Until now, I'd always believed we had the best police in the world. I didn't accept stories about corruption and fabricating evidence. But now . . .'

'Do you know the name of the officer?'

'The one who's been here before. Chief Inspector Stanhope.'

'Stanwick, do you mean?'

'Yes, yes, you know who I mean,' she said impatiently. 'And there was a sergeant with him, whom I didn't like at all. Absolutely no manners. And all this at eight o'clock in the morning. I ask you! Talk about the knock on the door and people being carted off for secret interrogation.'

'I do understand how you feel,' Rosa broke in, 'but you must try and keep calm. Presumably he's been taken to Havenbridge police station to be charged, which means he'll appear in court there later today. I'll find out the position and come down.'

Three phone calls later, Rosa was ready to depart. She left a message for Stanwick saying she was on her way and would he please ensure that Adrian's court appearance was held back until her arrival. She then left a similar message on the clerk of the court's answering machine. When she called her own office expecting once more to be greeted by an answering machine, she heard instead Ben's cheerful voice.

'Don't worry, Miss E,' he said when she had explained the situation. 'I'll let Mr Snaith know as soon as he comes in and also tell Steph.'

'I'm supposed to be in court at Ealing this afternoon, Ben. Can you get that put off or find somebody to stand in for me?'

'No problem, Miss E, I'll see to everything.'

Rosa thanked him and not for the first time blessed the day that Ben, newly released from a spell of youth custody, had joined the firm as a very probationary clerk. From that uncertain beginning he had graduated to highly valued member of the staff, with a record of utter reliability.

As she wove her way out of London against the incoming morning traffic, her mind was fully occupied with thoughts of what lay ahead. It was obvious that the police had come up with further evidence to justify the charge of murder. Her guess was that the laboratory had found something which tilted the scales against him. It could be blood on Adrian's clothing which matched that of the dead man. She wished she knew how far she could rely on what he had told her. He had either behaved with incredible stupidity or had told lie after lie. She decided that she had best reserve judgement until she had arrived in Havenbridge.

She parked in the police station yard and went inside.

'Will you please tell Detective Chief Inspector Stanwick that I'm here and wish to see my client. I'm Adrian Pickard's solicitor.'

The stout, balding officer at the enquiry desk gave her a calm, untroubled look. He was used to all sorts and reckoned he could deal with most.

'And your name?' he asked.

'Rosa Epton.'

'If you take a seat, Miss Epton, I'll find out if the chief inspector is available.'

'I assume my client *is* somewhere on the premises?'

'I'm sure the chief inspector will be able to tell you,' he replied in his anodyne tone.

He's more calming than a tankful of fish, Rosa reflected. He ambled away and she sat down on a bench against the wall to await events. When he reappeared it was to say that Chief Inspector Stanwick was otherwise engaged for the moment, but that she was welcome to speak to her client if she wished. She decided not to join issue over the fact that it was being made to sound as if she was being granted a special favour, whereas she regarded it as her right.

She followed the officer out of the reception area and down a corridor that led to the cells. Adrian was in the last one on the left. He was sitting dejectedly on a wooden bench holding a plastic cup in one hand. He put it down on the floor and jumped to his feet as she entered.

'You must wish you had never met me,' he said by way of greeting. 'I suppose Margaret called you. Is she in a terrible state?'

'No more than one would expect. She sounded more angry and indignant than anything else. Have you been charged yet?'

He nodded. 'With murder. It's unbelievable. Me, charged with murder.'

'In respect of Atherly's death?'

'Yes.'

'Have the police said what further evidence has come into their hands to warrant the charge?'

'Stanwick said they had proof that I met Atherly up at the school on the evening he died. But it isn't true.'

'What proof?'

'He didn't say.'

Rosa frowned. She would have expected the evidence, whatever

141

it was, to have been put to Adrian for his reaction. So why hadn't it?

'You must have some idea what it is?'

'I swear I don't,' he said wearily. 'What'll happen in court this morning?'

'There'll be a remand.' She paused. 'I think you must expect to be kept in custody.'

'But they can't do that. Margaret needs me. She can't be left on her own. You must tell the court that,' he said urgently.

'I'll do my best, but I'm not optimistic.'

He closed his eyes and clutched his head as if the world had given a convulsive lurch.

The cell door opened and Sergeant Travis stood there.

'Time to go across to court,' he said.

Adrian followed him as if the gallows were their actual destination. Rosa made her own way to the court which was on the opposite side of the road.

'I received your message,' the clerk said as she took her place. 'I'm glad you managed to get here so quickly as we don't have a long list for this morning and the chairman wants to get away as soon as possible. Will you be making any applications?' Before Rosa could reply, he went on, 'I'm sure the justices will grant legal aid. Ordinarily the defence would go to a local solicitor, but as you've been representing Pickard from the outset, there won't be any problem giving you the certificate.'

'I shall also be applying for bail,' Rosa said.

The clerk pulled a face. 'I think that's likely to be a non-starter. After all, murder is murder and though I know bail is sometimes granted, I doubt whether my justices will exercise their discretion in your favour.'

Which means, Rosa reflected, that you'll advise them not to.

A rather corpulent young man came hurrying into court and sat down next to Rosa. He had a pink, moist appearance.

'I'm Vokin from the CPS,' he said. 'I presume you're Miss Epton?'

'I am.'

'Everything's straightforward, isn't it?'

'Perfectly as far as I'm concerned,' Rosa replied, blandly.

'Good-o. I'd better have a quick look at my papers. All I know at the moment is that your client has been charged

142

with murder. It's probably all I need to know at this stage, isn't it?'

'You mean you're not ready to open your case and call witnesses?'

For a second he quivered like a startled animal, then he grinned. 'You had me worried for a second. Once we've served the statements, I imagine you'll agree to a paper committal?'

'That'll depend,' Rosa said. 'I don't agree to paper committals simply to save everyone's time.'

'No, of course not,' he said hastily. 'But contesting a case in the magistrates' court which can only be tried in the crown court isn't usually very good tactics.'

'It is if the magistrates decide there's no case to answer.'

'But how often does that happen?'

'Often enough to keep the prosecution on its toes,' Rosa remarked. Teasing the prosecution was legitimate sport, especially when it was represented by the likes of Mr Vokin.

An usher called for silence and three magistrates filed in to take their seats on the bench.

The court's first business was to deal with applications, of which there were two. The first was by an hotelier for an extension of his drinks licence on behalf of a wedding reception to be held on his premises. His application was quickly granted and he departed, looking pleased. The second applicant was a frail old man who seemed to pop up from nowhere and said he was applying on behalf of Her Majesty for warrants of arrest against every member of parliament for high treason. His application was refused in the gentlest possible way and he departed apparently satisfied with his morning's work, assisted from the court by a buxom lady usher.

'We shan't see him again for another month,' the clerk whispered to Rosa with a smile. 'He's quite harmless and never takes up too much time. Would that all our advocates were as brief and to the point! Now we're ready for your case.'

Adrian came into court and the clerk read out the charge and explained that, if a prima facie case was established, he would be tried by a jury at the crown court. He was invited to sit down and Mr Vokin, who now looked even pinker and moister, heaved himself to his feet.

'I am asking for a remand in custody, your worships,' he said. 'The charge was only preferred this morning and there are still many enquiries to be made.' He stood blinking for a few moments, then abruptly sat down.

'Anything you wish to say to their worships, Miss Epton?' the clerk enquired.

Rosa rose to her feet and met the gaze of the three magistrates who sat with politely attentive expressions.

'I am in no position to resist the application for a remand, your worships, but I do wish to apply for bail. Gone are the days when such an application in a murder case was unthinkable. Indeed, in today's climate, magistrates are being constantly exhorted to be more liberal in their approach to bail, and that includes cases of murder. In the present case, the defendant has a fixed address and is perfectly prepared to give an undertaking to keep away from all witnesses and potential witnesses, should the prosecution be worried on that score. Moreover, he will surrender his passport and report daily to the police, if you feel those are desirable safeguards. Finally, I should like to mention that the defendant's wife is not in good health and is very dependent on her husband's presence in the home. When the time comes he will strenuously fight the charge, which he has denied from the outset.'

The chairman of the bench thanked her, then he and his two colleagues bent their heads together in whispered consultation. Rosa realised that her application had small chance of success. It required courage (if not a degree of rashness) to grant bail in a case where the victim had been done to death in a particularly brutal fashion. A remand in custody was much the safer course and would be beyond any criticism.

'We remand the defendant in custody,' the chairman announced and proceeded to give the court's stereotyped, but unanswerable, reasons for refusing bail.

Adrian threw Rosa a forlorn look as he left the dock. She was glad she had told him that she would see him before he was taken off to prison, if that happened to be the outcome. First, however, she wanted to speak to Stanwick and was determined to catch him before he disappeared. In the event it was he who approached her as she was thrusting papers into her briefcase.

'I'd like to have a word, Miss Epton,' he said.

'And I with you,' she replied.

'All right, you go first,' he said when they were seated in a small, uncomfortable room off the main lobby.

'I'd like to know what further evidence you have that supports a charge of murder.'

'I could say that you'll have to wait until the bundle of statements is served on you. You've no right to the information at this stage.'

'Oh, well, if you're going to stand on protocol . . .'

'I didn't say that.'

'I must have misunderstood you. So, do we talk or glare at one another?'

Both of them were well aware that co-operation was a two-way affair. If he wanted Rosa's help, he had to be prepared to offer something in exchange. Rosa waited, almost able to read his mind.

'The answer to your question is that we've found a notebook in which Atherly used to jot things down. The final entry shows that he was going to meet your client at Warren Hall School at ten o'clock on the evening he was killed. It clearly links your client to the scene of the crime.'

'Do you have the notebook?'

'Not with me.'

'I don't suppose there'd be any objection to my examining it?'

'I'd have to consult the CPS.'

'Where was it found?'

'Mrs Atherly came across it and handed it to Sergeant Travis.'

'How long has it been in your possession?'

'Since the day before yesterday. Look, Miss Epton, I'm not prepared to answer endless questions.'

'Just one more,' Rosa said with a disarming smile. 'Can you remember the precise wording of this entry?'

'It said, "Sun eve", obviously meaning Sunday evening, "Mr P, W.H., 10".'

'Mr P, W.H., 10,' Rosa repeated.

'Mr Pickard, Warren Hall, ten o'clock,' Stanwick said quickly.

Rosa nodded thoughtfully. 'I'll be most interested to see the entry for myself,' she said.

Her immediate reaction was that it fell far short of being conclusive evidence against Adrian, if indeed it was evidence at all. It was like somebody producing a ticket to prove they had been to the cinema. It wasn't in itself evidence of the fact at all.

But if Stanwick chose to believe it was a vital piece of evidence, let him. For the time being, at least.

Stanwick broke in on her thoughts. 'We're still awaiting the lab report on your client's clothing,' he said. 'Now, may I ask you a question? When we arrested Pickard this morning, he indicated that he would like to make a statement about the burglary charge, but that he must speak to you first. If the two charges are in some way connected . . .' He let the sentence tail off.

'They are and they aren't,' Rosa said after a pause. 'As I told the court, the murder charge will be contested every inch of the way. As to the other, he'll admit breaking into the school, though not to commit any of the offences specified in the Act. He went there to study school photographs,' Rosa went on. 'He believes that Stephen Willett, the boy who disappeared and was presumed to have been murdered was, in fact, his father . . .'

An expression as concentrated as that of a cat watching a mousehole came over Stanwick's face. When she finished speaking, he said, 'And do you believe he really is Willett's son?'

'I think it's probable.'

'If it's true, it opens up a large can of worms. I've heard about the Willett case, of course, though heaven knows if there's any record of Price's trial lying around in anyone's archives. There's an old boy named Bob Vicary who's now in his eighties and lives in Dover. He remembers the case. He used to be in the force and was a constable at Greenborough when it happened. He comes over to headquarters once in a while for a pint of beer and a spot of reminiscence. He loves trotting out his memories. I know he thinks Price was a lucky fellow not to have been hanged. He's sure that he murdered the boy and managed to conceal the body.' He gave Rosa a hard stare. 'You realise that the press have only to get a whiff of this for them to descend like a swarm of bees.'

'Yes, but if it's my client's defence to the burglary charge – and it *does* explain his interest in the school – I can't help what the press do.'

'It'll reopen old wounds. I imagine Mr Thurston would sooner his school was struck by an earthquake than by this.'

'Have you considered the possibility that Bruce Thurston is a murderer? You've just provided the motive,' Rosa said, slightly nettled by Stanwick's implied appeal to her finer instincts.

'As far as I'm concerned, Miss Epton, your *client* is the murderer, possibly a double murderer.'

'I very much doubt whether a jury will agree with you. He'll be acquitted, just as Walter Price was.'

'As far as I'm concerned, the past is simply a red herring. If I may say so, you're just muddying the waters.'

Rosa bit her lip. She had believed him to be more open-minded than appeared to be the case, though she could see that what she had told him was hardly welcome news on the day Adrian had been charged with Joe Atherly's murder. She was not, however, in the business of offering him sympathy. Any more than he was to her.

'Well, Chief Inspector,' she said when the silence that had fallen had become oppressive, 'my client is ready to make a statement under caution on the lines I've indicated.'

'About the burglary?'

'Yes.'

'What about the murder?'

'Possibly a short statement vigorously denying the charge.'

'I was planning to question him under caution. There are one or two points that require clearing up.'

'But you've already charged him.'

Stanwick looked embarrassed. 'I realise that Sergeant Travis rather jumped the gun over the actual charging. It shouldn't have taken place until I was ready.' He gave Rosa a rueful glance.

'What do you wish to question him about?'

'Concerning his movements on the Sunday evening.'

'I'll let you know,' Rosa said, pushing back her chair and standing up. 'I need to speak to him first.'

'If you come over to the station, you can see him now.'

The officer who escorted Adrian into her presence retired from the room, only to stand guard outside the door where he cast a solid shadow across the frosted glass panel.

'I thought you must have left,' he said reproachfully.

'I told you I'd see you before I went.'

'I know, but — '

'Forget it,' Rosa said, not unkindly. 'I've been talking to Stanwick and have told him what you were doing at the school that night.'

'Does he believe me?'

'He didn't say one way or the other. But I said you were willing to make a statement about the incident.'

'What, today?'

'The sooner the better. Stanwick also wants to question you about your movements on the evening of Joe Atherly's death. Strictly he's out of order, and any interrogation places you in a dilemma. You've lied to the police about what you did that evening and we now have to decide on the best line to take. If they're in a position to prove your lie – for example, if they have a witness who recognised you in the pub where you were drinking or have found someone who took your car number while you were dealing with the dog you'd run over – then the longer you maintain your lie, the worse it could be.'

'Can't you find out how much the police know?' he asked desperately.

'We shan't know until they serve their witnesses' statements on us. I suspect that Stanwick may already be regretting having told me as much as he did.'

'So you think it'll be better if I admit I was out that evening and the business about the dog? Anyway, what *did* Stanwick tell you?'

'That they'd found a notebook at Atherly's house, the last entry in which could be interpreted as a reference to meeting you at Warren Hall at ten o'clock on Sunday evening.'

Adrian stared at her aghast. 'But that's preposterous.'

'Any admission that you were out around that time will lend credence to Joe Atherly's written note.'

'Won't the police be bound to ask why I lied to them about my movements?'

'The answer to that is you panicked after running over the dog. Your conscience told you that you should have tried to find the owner, but you knew the families who lived at the encampment had the reputation of being a trouble-making lot and you wished to avoid an encounter.'

'That's true.'

'And it's the reason you didn't tell Stanwick the truth when he first asked you about your movements.' Adrian nodded. 'And why you lied about the clothes you'd been wearing.'

'Yes,' he said eagerly.

'You wouldn't be the first innocent person to panic and lie to the police,' Rosa remarked. 'One of the hypocrisies of our criminal justice system is that innocent people need never fear telling the truth. The other side of that coin being that a proven lie is the equivalent of guilt. In my experience, innocent people often lie or conceal the truth when they're caught up in police enquiries.'

She observed Adrian's unhappy expression as his thoughts wrestled with one another. Eventually he gave a helpless shrug.

'It seems I'm sunk whatever I do,' he said.

'That's defeatist talk. I'm hopeful we can show the murder charge to be totally misconceived.'

'You mean, you know who killed Joe Atherly?'

'I believe the same person murdered both Wells and Atherly and that I'm on the way to finding out who it is. That's all I'm going to say for the moment.'

26

It took over two hours to record Adrian's statements. One dealing with the burglary incident, the other with the murder charge. When she finally left Havenbridge, Rosa was happy to note that her client was in considerably better heart than he had been when she arrived. She was also relieved that by coming clean about his movements on the fateful Sunday evening he had removed an ethical problem which she had seen looming. Namely, that of a lawyer being asked to put forward a defence which the client had admitted was untrue. It was a complication she could well do without.

She had spoken briefly on the telephone to Margaret and had promised to call in at Greenborough on her way back to London. It was near enough three thirty when she arrived in the village and parked outside the post office.

As she approached the front door, she could see Margaret sitting at a card table in the window and recalled her godmother's recourse to playing patience at times of stress.

'I never go anywhere without a pack of cards,' she had once

said to Rosa. 'A pack of cards and a bottle of eau de cologne. Give me those and you can abandon me in a desert.'

It was with a certain feeling of dread that she rang the bell, for she was not relishing the meeting. She soon realised, however, that she had underestimated her godmother's resilience. Her mood of anger and indignation had given way to one of calm acceptance. Not for the first time Rosa reflected that old people were often much better at absorbing emotional shock than the young.

'Would you care for something to drink?' Margaret asked, as Rosa followed her into the sitting room. 'I've been playing patience, but was about to stop for a cup of tea.'

'I'd love one too,' Rosa said. 'Let me make it.'

'I can do it perfectly well, thank you, dear. It may have been a confusing day, but I can still put a kettle on.'

Rosa followed her into the kitchen. 'Adrian's bearing up well and sent you his love,' she said.

'I don't pretend to know everything that's been happening, though I do know rather more than Adrian suspects. There's always someone in a village to keep you abreast of the underside of life.'

'What exactly have you heard?' Rosa asked.

'I know he was found on the premises of Warren Hall School and was arrested by the police.'

'Do you know what he was doing there?'

'It's something to do with his past, isn't it? He's obsessed with finding out about his parentage and he believes the school played a part. There was the boy who disappeared and was believed to have been murdered.' She fixed Rosa with a steady look. 'If digging into his past made him happy, I wasn't going to interfere. I wasn't even going to bother him with questions. I've reached an age when I don't particularly wish to know everything about those around me. I often think that reserve and reticence are becoming obsolete virtues and more's the pity.' She finished making the tea. 'You can carry the tray, if you want to do something to help.' They returned to the sitting room and sat down. She poured out and handed Rosa a cup and said emphatically, 'Of one thing I am sure, Adrian's not a murderer. The police have made a hideous mistake in arresting him and I can never feel quite the same towards them again.' Then in a matter-of-fact tone she asked, 'How long is it likely to be before he's home again?'

'I don't think there's any hope of bail at the moment. Once the prosecution statements have been served, I'll know the strength of their case and its weaknesses.'

'Do you think he'd like me to visit him while he's in prison?'

'I'm sure he'd not want you to go if it'd be a great strain.'

'It's bound to be that, but I'll certainly go if it'll help his morale. I don't want people in the village to think I've deserted him in his hour of need. They think enough odd things about me as it is.'

'Well, you are a rather unusual pair,' Rosa said with a faint smile.

'I'm very much aware of it. The fact is, however, that we've both got what we want from our marriage. I have companionship, even if it's temporarily snatched away, and Adrian has found stability for the first time in his life. Or he had until this morning, poor love. He had always hankered after settling down in a village and running a store and I've helped him achieve that.' She gave Rosa a defiant look. 'I don't know whether you know, but sub post offices are an excellent investment at the present time.'

'I'm delighted to hear it,' Rosa said. After a short silence she went on, 'I suppose it's too early for the village to have reacted to Adrian's arrest?'

'Mrs Ives, who serves in the post office, has already phoned to express what she referred to as her condolences. She said that Adrian was far too much of a gentleman to be a murderer, though I feel that shows a certain naïvety on her part. And I've seen a number of people staring at the cottage from the road, presumably in the hope of catching sight of me up to something suspicious.'

'I suppose there were rumours going around before as to who killed Atherly?'

Margaret pursed her lips. 'Sir Denzil Cuckfield seems to have been the favourite.' Observing Rosa's expression she added, 'You don't seem very surprised.'

'I'm trained not to show surprise. And, anyway, after a dozen years in a criminal practice, there's not much left to cause one surprise.'

'You're too young to become a hardened cynic,' Margaret said in a tone of admonition.

Rosa laughed. 'Tell me, what's the theory about Sir Denzil?'

'He's not popular, and with a lot of people I'm sure that suspecting him is the equivalent of sticking pins into a wax doll.'

'What motive is he supposed to have had?'

'There's a suggestion that Atherly was blackmailing him. It's hinted he knew a dark secret in Sir Denzil's past. It's certainly true they've known each other for the best part of sixty years. Both grew up in Greenborough. I don't think villages are much different today from what they were a hundred years ago. They still thrive on gossip and rumours.'

There was a knock on the front door and Margaret let out a sigh. Turning back to Rosa, she said, 'Go and see who it is, dear, and say I'm too tired to receive visitors.'

Rosa went out into the tiny hall and opened the door. A pleasant-looking woman of around forty stared at her in surprise.

'I only called to see how Mrs Pickard is,' she said. 'I'm Mrs Ives and I help out at the post office.'

'I'm Mr Pickard's solicitor,' Rosa said. 'I also happen to be Mrs Pickard's goddaughter.'

'I've heard Mr Pickard mention your name.' She peered past Rosa into the hall. 'How is Mrs Pickard?'

'She's resting. It's been an exhausting day for her.'

'Will you be staying with her?'

'No, I have to get back to London this evening.'

'And Mr Pickard?'

'He's being kept in custody at the moment.'

Mrs Ives nodded. 'I wonder if Mrs Pickard would like me to bring her in some supper. I know Mr Pickard usually does the cooking, but I can easily bring something in if it'll help.'

'That's most kind of you, but I think she's just going to have a bowl of soup and go to bed early. Perhaps tomorrow she'd be grateful for something.'

'I'll look in on my way to work and see if there's anything I can do, so don't you worry about her. We all like Mrs Pickard. She's a real down-to-earth lady.'

Mrs Ives seemed a genuinely kind person, even though Rosa suspected she was trying to get in on the act. In the circumstances, she didn't see why she shouldn't make use of Mrs Ives' presence on the doorstep to take further soundings of village opinion.

'Can you hang on a moment,' she said. 'I'll just go and see how my godmother is.' She darted back inside the cottage, told

152

Margaret who the visitor was and returned after firmly closing the sitting room door behind her. 'I gather you believe Adrian Pickard is innocent.'

'I'm quite sure he never did it,' Mrs Ives declared stoutly.

'Do you have any evidence to support your view?'

'I don't need evidence, I just know. Mr Pickard is a real gentleman. He'd be incapable of killing anyone, even a slippery rogue like Joe Atherly.'

'You don't have a very high opinion of Atherly?'

'I know it's what my father thought of him and he'd grown up with Joe. Mind you, he'd never done *me* any harm, but I've always felt sorry for his wife.' She paused and appeared to be searching for the right word. 'He was what you call an opportunitist.' She frowned. 'Is that what I mean?'

'I think it's opportunist,' Rosa said. 'Do you know if he had any enemies?'

'I don't know about actual enemies, but I don't think he had any friends either. Not real friends, that is. He'd lived in Greenborough all his life and knew everything that had ever happened here. I expect you've heard about the boy who disappeared from Warren Hall back in the thirties?' Rosa nodded and Mrs Ives went on, 'It was Joe Atherly who shopped Wally Price. He told the police that Wally had interfered with the boy. My dad knew Wally and said he'd never have done such a thing. Luckily, Wally got off.'

'So you don't believe he murdered the boy?'

'Not from what my dad said. More likely to have been Joe himself.'

'Isn't it possible the boy was never killed at all?'

'Some thought one thing, some the other. It was all long before I was born. But the village still has its memories.'

'I'm certainly very glad you believe in my client's innocence,' Rosa said. 'You can let it be known that he completely denies the charge and will fight it all the way. So, who do you think did murder Joe Atherly?'

Mrs Ives threw Rosa an anxious look. 'This is just a doorstep conversation, isn't it? You're not going to pass it on to the police?'

'You have my word on that.'

'Most folk in the village believe that Joe was murdered because he'd been digging into someone's past and found out things the someone didn't want brought to light.'

'Would the someone be Sir Denzil Cuckfield?'

Mrs Ives glanced quickly about her, then gave a swift nod. 'The general belief is that Joe was lured to the school in order to cast suspicion on Mr Thurston, but nobody thinks he did it.'

'I wonder if the murderer was aware that Mr Thurston had returned from Wales that day?' Rosa said in a musing tone.

'You take my word for it, neither Mr Pickard nor Mr Thurston killed Joe. It was someone else,' she added ominously. She glanced at her watch. 'I must dash or my husband won't find his tea ready when he gets home. Don't forget to tell Mrs Pickard I'll look in tomorrow morning. And don't you worry, I'll keep a good eye on her.'

When Rosa returned to the sitting room, she found Margaret asleep in her chair. But she awoke before Rosa had taken a couple of steps.

'What time is it?'

'Nearly five thirty.'

'Has that woman left?'

'Yes, but she intends keeping an eye on you.'

'I don't want anyone's eyes kept on me,' Margaret said emphatically.

Half an hour later Rosa was on her way back to London. It had been a long and exhausting day, but a far from wasted one. Her conversation with Mrs Ives had been useful in giving her an idea of where village loyalties lay. There was always a certain satisfaction in casting unpopular figures as villains. In Sir Denzil's case, however, there could be more to it than mere low standing in the popularity stakes.

She was now quite certain that the vital clue to the two deaths which had taken place lay firmly in the past.

27

'Who have you been talking to on the telephone?' Sir Denzil Cuckfield asked his wife.

She had just reached the bottom of the staircase when he came out of his study.

'I thought you'd gone out, dear,' she said.

'Well, you can see I haven't. Who were you talking to?'

'Martin.'

'You know he doesn't like being phoned at the ministry unless it's urgent.'

'I called the flat to speak to Sylvia and Martin answered. He has an important speech to make tomorrow and stayed at home to prepare it.'

Sir Denzil frowned as he digested the information.

'What did you want to speak to Sylvia about?'

'Robert's been off school and I phoned to find out if he was better.' Robert, aged ten, was the older of Martin's two children.

'And is he better?' the grandfather asked.

'Yes, he's going back tomorrow.'

'What else did Martin have to say?'

'He's very busy and doesn't know when he'll come down to see us.'

'You were talking to him for over ten minutes,' Sir Denzil said accusingly. He had always resented the fact that Martin was closer to his mother than to him. In his view, sons should take after their fathers and daughters could take after anyone they liked.

'You don't mind my talking to him, do you?' his wife asked.

'Of course I don't. I just wonder what you have to talk about.'

'He was asking whether there'd been any further developments in the Atherly case and I told him that Mr Pickard had been arrested and charged.'

'And about time, too. I've been made aware of scurrilous rumours circulating in the village and have let it be known that I shan't hesitate to issue writs for slander if they continue.'

'Is that why you didn't go down to the village this morning?'

'Partly,' he said grudgingly. 'I don't like people staring at me and tittle-tattling behind my back. What's more, I won't put up with it.'

'You have a pair of broad shoulders,' his wife said peaceably.

'Broad shoulders be damned! I'm not going to have my good name besmirched by gossip-mongers.' He glared at his wife. 'I'm proud to say that I've never courted cheap popularity.'

Joyce Cuckfield refrained from comment. She was well aware how the village regarded her husband and did her quiet best to try and redress the balance.

'What was Martin's reaction to news of Pickard's arrest?' her husband asked abruptly.

'I don't think he said anything in particular.'

'Of course he must have.' When his wife still remained silent, he burst out. 'You really can be a most infuriating woman at times.'

Joyce Cuckfield had been used to her husband's tirades all her married life and reacted much as a rock pounded by heavy seas.

'Lunch should be ready quite soon,' she remarked as she turned to go toward the kitchen.

Though they had been married for thirty-seven years, she was still able to baffle him by her response to certain situations. Her appearance of being a somewhat weak and nervous person was nothing more than a façade behind which lurked a stubborn and often determined woman. Though he would never admit it, she had soon got the measure of her husband and had never lost it. The quiet country girl he had married had never been overawed at becoming a Cuckfield. She had grown up on a farm in Derbyshire. Her parents had both been in their forties when she was born and had long since died. They had been devoted to Joyce, and she had returned their affection.

Denzil Cuckfield had met her at a dance when he was staying with friends in the district. He was then thirty-one and ready for marriage. Joyce had seemed to have all the makings of a perfect partner. Pretty, polite and submissive and the daughter of respectable farming folk.

Things, however, had not worked out as he had expected. But then whose marriage ever does, he reflected?

Closing his study door behind him, he went over to the window and gazed across the garden to the meadows beyond. In the distance he could see the gabled roof of Warren Hall School. It was sixty years since he had first gone there as a boarder. Sixty years of kaleidoscopic change in the world outside.

Suddenly he took an angry swipe at a bluebottle fitfully buzzing away the end of its life.

28

It was customary for the staff of Warren Hall to meet under the chairmanship of the headmaster on the day before the boys returned for a new term. The agenda was apt to be lengthy and the meeting to last for most of an afternoon. The main topics were changes to the syllabus and any revision of school rules. Nothing, however, was precluded.

They sat at the table in the staff dining room with Mr Thurston at the head and the rest of them, more or less in order of seniority, ranged on either side of him.

'Doesn't seem as if she's back,' one of the youngest masters whispered to his equally youthful colleague, referring to Mrs Thurston.

'Nor's the junior PE teacher,' replied the other with a knowing smile.

'Poor old Bruce. He's looking pretty hollow-eyed.'

'Don't think that has anything to do with wifey's absence. More likely to be due to the outbreak of sudden death all around him.' He gave his companion a sly grin. 'He can hardly avoid mentioning it.'

This exchange had taken place while they were waiting for the meeting to begin, but it was a long two hours later that the headmaster did, in fact, make reference to events which were uppermost in all their minds.

'There is one final matter before we disperse,' he said, glancing about him with a grave expression. 'Those of you who have kept in touch with newspapers during the school holidays will doubtless be aware of two sudden deaths which have occurred on school property. One was of a man named Harry Wells. Nobody seems to know what he was doing in Greenborough and as yet nobody has been charged in connection with his death. He had been coshed and then drowned. The second unfortunate victim was Joe Atherly. He had worked at the school for over sixty years and will be greatly missed. His body was found at the back of the cricket shed . . .'

'Is it true that matron discovered it?' one of the youthful two enquired with a barely-suppressed grin.

The headmaster frowned angrily. 'Matron had left her bicycle in the shed during the holidays and found the body when she went to retrieve the machine on her return. As you can imagine, it was a terrible shock to her, so please don't let us have any jocular remarks. As I was about to say, and as most of you will probably know, Mr Pickard, Greenborough's postmaster, has been charged with Atherly's murder. I expect most of you also knew Mr Pickard, which doesn't make things any pleasanter. I fear very much that these two deaths on the school doorstep are bound to preoccupy the boys' minds and I'm relying on each of you to discourage any morbid talk and speculation. I shall come down very hard on any boy I find indulging in idle gossip. There's a term's work to be got through and the fewer distractions, the better. Is that quite clear?' he asked, glancing from face to face.

'What do you want us to say, headmaster, to boys who come straight out with comments and questions about the murders?' asked the younger of the two youthful masters. 'It seems to me it's bound to happen.'

'You will say,' Thurston observed in a forceful tone, 'that you are not prepared to enter into any discussion of the matter and that if you hear another word you'll report the boy to me. In any event I have phoned all the parents personally and assured them of their boys' safety.'

'Are you proposing to say anything to the boys themselves?' asked Miss Ensor, who taught the bottom class.

'Yes, after prayers tomorrow evening. I shall tell them it's a non-subject and anyone disobeying the edict will be severely punished.'

The meeting broke up and the two youngest masters, who shared a flat in the village, left together.

'Nothing we do or say will stop the boys discussing what's happened,' observed one.

'I know,' said the other. 'It'd be much better to tell them that for two days they're not allowed to talk about anything else. That would give them time to get it out of their systems.' He paused before adding, 'He's obviously concerned for the school's reputation. But why be so tetchy with us? It's almost as if old Bruce has got something to hide.'

'I was thinking the same thing. I imagine the police must have questioned him about the two deaths. Maybe he's not yet in the clear.'

'But they've already charged that bloke from the post office.'

'Charged him, yes, but only with Atherly's death. And anyway, that doesn't mean he did it.'

'You've watched too much TV.'

'Possibly, but I still think old Bruce was distinctly uncomfortable. He certainly isn't the man he used to be. I believe he doesn't want any discussion of what's happened because he's frightened of what may come out.' He paused and a smile spread across his face. 'I'd love to have seen matron's expression when she discovered the body.'

'A look of distaste registering seven on the Richter Scale would be my guess.'

'Serve the old cow right! I've not forgiven her for telling Bruce that I gave that snide little creature in Four a good boot up his backside. She's lucky I didn't give her one too.'

'Ah, well, let's go and drink to a jolly term.'

'With further murders as non-subjects.'

29

Mr Seale of the CPS wore a beleaguered look as he faced Chief Inspector Stanwick and Sergeant Travis across his desk.

'I wish I'd seen these statements earlier,' he said with a sigh.

'Pickard only made them after his court appearance yesterday,'

Stanwick replied. 'I sent them over by hand as soon as they'd been copied.'

'Yes, yes, I know it's not your fault, but I wish he'd spoken out earlier. In respect of the burglary charge, that is.'

'I don't see that it could have affected your advice to charge him with Atherly's murder, sir,' Travis said aggressively. 'Anyway, if you ask me, that statement is a load of old cobblers. I don't believe for a moment he broke into the school merely to look at photographs.'

'What then was his motive for forcing an entry?' the solicitor enquired.

Travis glowered at him. 'Whatever it was, I'm sure it wasn't as innocent as he'd have us believe.'

'Is that also your view, Chief Inspector?'

'I doubt whether he could have invented such a remarkable story.'

'So you think it's true?'

'Regretfully, yes.'

'I totally disagree,' Travis broke in.

Stanwick gave his sergeant a quelling glance and went on, 'Though the statement about the burglary has no relevance to the murder charge, I feel pretty certain the defence will seek to introduce it.'

'I'm quite sure they will,' Seale remarked. 'I've not personally come across Miss Epton, but she has a formidable reputation. I think these two statements are a measure of her tactical skill. The one about the burglary is certainly an embarrassment to us.'

'If you ask me,' Travis growled, 'the fact that Pickard didn't make it at the first opportunity is proof of its fabrication. He's been in Greenborough long enough to have heard about the boy who disappeared from Warren Hall and it was perfectly easy for him to weave himself into the story.'

'But why? What was his motive?' the solicitor asked.

'I don't know, but I'm darned sure he was up to no good.' After a pause, he added, 'Anyway, the murder charge is the important one and we've got enough against him on that to satisfy any jury.'

'I wish I could share your confidence,' Seale said with a small superior smile that served only to fuel Travis' simmering irritation. 'My own view is that we have a reasonably solid-looking case, but will it stand up to cross-examination?'

'Pickard has got to explain why he lied about his movements that Sunday evening and why he tried to palm me off with clothes he'd not been wearing,' Stanwick said.

'He does so in his statement,' Seale remarked.

'You find that plausible, sir?'

'I don't find it wholly implausible,' Seale replied. 'Don't misunderstand me, Chief Inspector, all I'm saying is that I wish I'd known earlier what Pickard was going to allege. I really do feel that his statement about the burglary requires more consideration.' He gave his visitors a melancholy stare. 'It's rather like a grenade with the pin already pulled out.'

'It was your decision that we had sufficient evidence to charge Pickard with murder,' Travis said hotly. 'You felt that the notebook I found at Atherly's house clinched the case.'

Seale sighed. 'I'm afraid I may have allowed myself to be bulldozed into agreeing that Pickard should be charged on the strength of that additional bit of evidence. I was rather rushed into a decision. Let's hope there's no occasion to repent at leisure.' Turning to Stanwick he went on, 'How soon will you be able to let me have the witnesses' statements on which we're going to rely?'

'We're working flat out on them now, but there are still a lot of loose ends to be tied up.'

'Well, please bear in mind, Chief Inspector, that Havenbridge is one of the more demanding courts in the area. The clerk is not exactly a friend of the CPS and the justices can be unduly outspoken on the subject of delay.' He let out another sigh. 'What with that and Miss Epton defending, we could be in for a bumpy ride.'

On this uneasy note the meeting ended.

'Ours wouldn't be a bad job if we didn't have to deal with lawyers,' Travis observed sourly as he and Stanwick left the building.

30

Rosa was looking forward to the weekend, after a busy, even arduous, period of work.

Peter had flown to Vienna for a meeting with Japanese clients and wouldn't be back before Tuesday. Though she would miss him, she was looking forward to having time to herself.

On Saturday she would do a week's shopping for food in the morning and then give her flat a thorough clean. She had been told that pushing a vacuum cleaner around was an excellent therapy for those whose intellectual powers needed a rest. Personally, she had never found it other than a chore and an utterly boring one at that.

Given good weather on Sunday, she proposed to drive down to Sussex and take a long walk on the Downs. Walking was something she did find therapeutic. Many was the knot she had unravelled, the problem she had satisfactorily solved, while putting one foot in front of the other and gently vibrating her brain cells.

As a result of her various researches, she now thought she knew the identity of the murderer, but so far she had no proof. She was hopeful that her Sunday walk would show her how the fruits of her research could be converted into hard evidence.

Her plans for the weekend were conditional on Margaret not needing her support. When she phoned on Saturday morning, her godmother told her to put the Pickards out of her mind for two days.

'If you're sure you don't need me,' Rosa had said.

'I'm more than sure. Everyone in the village is being most kind. To be quite truthful, too kind. I feel like a harvest festival with all the fruit and flowers that have been sent. The only reason for you to come down would be to take back a hundredweight of cooking apples.'

'Have you decided whether to visit Adrian in prison?'

'I'm still thinking about it.'

'Any fresh rumours going about the village?'

'Everyone still seems to have it in for Sir Denzil. He's almost been turned into a pantomine demon, poor man.' She paused. 'I say poor man, but perhaps he isn't.'

'The village clearly doesn't think so.'

Nor, indeed, did Rosa, although she said nothing to Margaret. She believed it was he who had killed both Harry Wells and Joe Atherly to prevent a scandal breaking. It seemed probable that both of them had been threatening blackmail, with Joe, the opportunist, putting on further pressure after Wells' death. As Rosa saw it, the common feature of the two cases was their reach into the past. Atherly had been a teenage employee at the school in the early thirties and Harry Wells' mother had been Wally Price's girl-friend at the same period.

And the third person who had been around then was Sir Denzil Cuckfield, himself a pupil at Warren Hall.

It was, she felt, a question of fitting the pieces together correctly.

She had just finished speaking to Margaret and was about to go out shopping when the telephone rang.

It was Peter calling from Vienna. Was she all right? Was she missing him? Would she have dinner with him on Tuesday? Having said yes to all three questions, she enquired after his Japanese clients.

'We went to *Tosca* last night. They were determined to go to an opera.'

'Did they enjoy it?'

'Yes, in a bemused sort of way. It was either Puccini last night or Wagner this evening.'

'I'm sure you made the right choice. To spring Wagner on the unsuspecting is a terrible risk.'

'Especially *Parsifal*.'

Rosa was glad when Saturday reached its end. The flat was certainly cleaner, though she knew fresh dust had already begun to accumulate.

The weather forecast for Sunday was for a generally sunny day in the south-east, with strong winds and occasional showers.

She set out around nine thirty and reached her chosen destination, a small village on the lee side of the South Downs, just under two hours later. She parked the car, changed her shoes and strode up a chalk track that led to a ridge along which she could walk with views of the English Channel on one side and rolling farmland on the other. It was time to pick up her thoughts where she had left them.

It was one thing to believe Sir Denzil Cuckfield was a murderer, another to prove it. Confrontation was out of the question, for he was not the sort of person at whom you flung accusations unless quite certain they would stick. Moreover, her first priority was to secure Adrian's acquittal, and to achieve that she didn't need to point the finger at anyone else, though that might help in the right circumstances. Sir Denzil, however, certainly presented a challenge to her detective instincts.

By the time she returned to her car, she had been walking for over two hours and according to her legs, for rather longer.

She was tired, but filled with a sense of mental and physical well-being. Moreover, she now saw the issues more clearly and knew what she had to do next.

Rosa was due in court on Monday morning and though she had the necessary papers with her, decided to stop off at the office on her way.

Stephanie, who was engaged in some quick titivation after her journey from the suburbs, raised a surprised eyebrow on seeing her.

'Forgotten something?' she enquired.

'No, but I want to make a phone call. Can you get me the CPS office that covers Havenbridge?'

'Anyone in particular?'

'The head of it. Perhaps you could find out his name for me, Steph. By the way, did you have a good weekend?'

'It was all right.' Stephanie had never been one for superlatives and Rosa smiled.

'And yours? Did you get the housework done?'

'Yes, and spent an enjoyable day in Sussex yesterday, recovering. I had a good five-mile walk.'

'I don't call that recovering,' Stephanie observed. 'I'll get this number for you.'

Rosa had not been in her room more than a couple of minutes when her phone buzzed.

'I have the person you want,' Stephanie announced. 'His name is Seale.'

'Miss Epton, is it?' a voice said with a slight note of apprehension.

'Yes. We haven't met, Mr Seale, but I'm defending in the case of Pickard.'

'Ah, yes, the murder. I'm afraid I'm not yet able to serve the statements on you. We're rather in the hands of the police on these occasions.'

'I know you're often blamed for delays which are not your fault,' Rosa said in her friendliest tone. 'But I'm not calling to complain, only to ask a favour. I understand a notebook belonging to the deceased man recently came into the possession of the police?'

'Yes, that's correct,' Seale replied cautiously.

'I imagine they've shown it to you?'

'Yes.'

'Would it be possible for me to have sight of it in advance of your sending me copies of statements and documentary exhibits?'

'Ah!' The monosyllable was long-drawn-out and Rosa waited for something to follow. 'I'm afraid it's not in my possession at the moment.' There followed an even longer pause before he spoke again. 'It's being examined at the laboratory. Purely a matter of routine.'

'That's very interesting.'

'Please don't read anything special into it. I felt it would be in everyone's interests to put the item in question beyond argument and dispute.'

'I'd like to see the report you receive,' Rosa said. 'Perhaps you'll let me know when you have it.'

The crown prosecutor made a somewhat equivocal reply and their conversation ended. It had, however, given Rosa greater food for thought than she had expected.

It was the next afternoon that Rosa decided to visit Mrs Wells again. She had spent the earlier part of the day at a court in south-east London, so it seemed a good idea to extend her journey to Woolwich before heading for home.

As she drew up outside 28 Volga Close she noticed that the curtains of the downstairs front room were pulled across the window. It might be, she thought, simply to protect the room from the sun's damaging rays. A lot of people did it.

After she had rung the bell and waited, then knocked and further waited, she stepped back and stared at the upstairs windows. While she was doing so the front door of the neighbouring house opened and a woman whom Rosa recognised from her previous visit appeared.

'It's Mrs Archer, isn't it?' she said with a hopeful smile.

'Yes and you're a solicitor. I remember your coming before.' She came across to where Rosa was standing. 'If you want Mrs Wells, I'm afraid you're too late. She went yesterday.'

'Went?'

'Passed away, poor old soul. Though in many ways it was a merciful release. I was just making a cup of tea, so why don't you come in. You see, it was me who found her.'

Rosa followed Mrs Archer into her house and into the kitchen at the rear.

'I happened to see you standing out there and recognised you at once. I never forget a face. Do you take milk and sugar?'

'Milk, please, but no sugar.'

'Like I say, it was me who discovered her. I'd been in early and she'd seemed all right, but when I went back to give her a spot of dinner, she was slumped in her chair and I could see at a glance she'd gone. It was just before one o'clock and I had made a shepherd's pie. She loved my shepherd's pie. Anyway, there I was holding a plate of pie and brussels sprouts and there was she gone to her rest. I phoned her doctor and later I got through to Brian, he's her eldest son, and he came over yesterday evening. They took her body away around seven. They wouldn't have if I'd not insisted, but I didn't like to think of her lying dead in her house all alone.'

'She was fortunate in having such a good neighbour,' Rosa remarked, when Mrs Archer's narrative came to a halt.

'I used to do what I could, especially after Harry's death. But, in my view, her other two sons should have done more, instead of relying on the likes of me to look after their mother. After all, I've got my own family. A husband and three kids. But they seemed to think that because I was next door, running in and out of their mother's house several times a day was no trouble. Anyway, it's all over now.'

'Had you known her a very long time?'

'We moved into the street six years ago, but it's only during the

166

last eighteen months she's gone downhill. Harry's death came as a terrible shock to her.'

'Did she ever talk about her past?'

Mrs Archer shook her head. 'No, she was funny in that way. It seemed as if she didn't want to talk about her early life. I asked her once if she had any brothers and sisters, and she said "no" and changed the subject. On another occasion I remember I was telling her about my childhood – of course, I was much younger than she was – but when I asked about hers, she shut up like a clam. I didn't want her to think I was prying, so I avoided the subject after that. But it did make me wonder . . . I'm sure there was something in her past she didn't want to be reminded of. I did once bring the subject up with Harry, but if he knew anything, he wasn't saying. He was an artful one was Harry, and he'd steal the coat off your back if he thought you wouldn't notice. His sort usually come to a sticky end.' She gave Rosa a quizzical look. 'I've not read that they've arrested anyone for his murder yet.'

'As far as I know, they haven't.'

'And I gather there's been another murder in the same village since.'

'Yes, a client of mine has been charged.'

'So that's what brought you back! You hoped Mrs Wells could tell you something.'

'It was possible,' Rosa said and got up to leave.

'My eldest boy fancies going in for the law,' Mrs Archer said suddenly. 'Perhaps you could have a talk with him sometime. He's got the brains; and the gift of the gab.'

Rosa was in no doubt from whom he'd inherited the latter. 'I'll leave you my card,' she said, 'and when he'd like to talk to somebody about a career in the law tell him to call me. By the way, how old is he?'

'Seventeen last birthday. His name's Perry. We called him that after Perry Mason. My husband and I both loved that series.'

As she drove back into central London, Rosa reflected that her visit to Volga Close had not been a complete waste of time. She had hoped that Mrs Wells could have been persuaded to confirm what her researches had brought to light, but it was not to be.

She wondered whether the murderer yet knew of Mrs Wells' death and how he'd react to the news. It was undoubtedly he who had phoned her after her son's death and pretended to be a friend of Harry's. It had sounded, the old lady had told Rosa, as if he were talking under water, which was clearly done to disguise his voice.

As she reviewed the facts, she found Sir Denzil still firmly in her sights. But how to clinch his guilt? That was the question.

31

Pedro, the male half of the husband and wife team currently employed at Greenborough Court, gave the breakfast gong a satisfying thwack. It was an old-fashioned gong with a penetrating sound and Sir Denzil insisted that it should be used to announce breakfast and dinner.

To Pedro it was another British absurdity, though he quite enjoyed giving it a good whack. It helped release a few of his pent-up emotions.

On this particular morning (it was the day after Rosa's visit to Volga Close) he struck the gong with extra vehemence and went back to the kitchen where Ana, his wife, was standing, eating a Danish pastry, for which she had developed a passion since arriving in England.

'They are down?' she enquired.

'No.' He sat down at the table and cut himself a thick slice of bread which he smothered in honey.

'All that honey,' his wife observed. 'It doesn't make you any sweeter.'

He ignored her and went on eating.

'I go and look round dining room door,' Ana said when she had finished a second Danish pastry. She padded out of the kitchen, only to return half a minute later. 'They are not down. Hit the gong again.'

'You could have.'

'It's your job.'

Pedro got up and left the kitchen, licking his fingers as he went. A few seconds later the sound of the gong once more reverberated through the house.

A further fifteen minutes went by and then Ana said in a decisive voice, 'I go and see.'

Her husband poured himself another cup of coffee and was about to drink it when he heard a shrill scream upstairs, followed by rapid footsteps descending. His wife appeared in the kitchen doorway, panting hard.

'Lady Cuckfield. I cannot wake her. I think she is dead.'

'Why you think she is dead?' Pedro asked suspiciously.

'You come,' she commanded.

He followed her up to the Cuckfields' bedroom on the first floor. It contained two single beds. One of them had been slept in, but was now empty; the other revealed the outline of a body beneath the duvet and Lady Cuckfield's neat grey head resting on the pillow. Pedro approached the bed cautiously and put out a hand to touch her forehead.

'Yes, she is dead,' he declared. He glanced at the bedside table on which there was a half-full glass of water and a bottle of tablets, which was almost empty.

'Her pills for sleeping,' Ana said, meeting her husband's look. She appeared close to tears and quite suddenly sank to her knees at the foot of the bed, crossed herself and began to pray in her native tongue.

'You phone police,' Pedro said.

She shook her head vigorously as she clambered to her feet. 'I phone doctor.'

'Go and phone someone,' her husband said impatiently.

'But where is Sir?' she asked, as if only now aware of Sir Denzil's absence.

'You phone. I look for him.'

A search of the house and the immediate vicinity, however, revealed no sign of its owner. His car was also missing.

By mid-morning, Martin Cuckfield had arrived from London and his mother's body had been removed to the mortuary for an autopsy. The family doctor said that the evidence pointed to her having died of an overdose of her prescribed sleeping tablets.

Of Sir Denzil, however, there was no sign at all.

'Have you any idea where your father might be?' Chief Inspector Stanwick asked.

Martin Cuckfield shook his head. He looked totally stunned by events.

'Or why your mother should have taken her life?' Stanwick went on.

He had been at the house when Martin arrived and had immediately sent to the kitchen for strong coffee. They were now sitting in Sir Denzil's study.

'I'm . . . I'm utterly devastated,' Martin said in a cracked voice. 'I can't believe it's happened. My life is shattered . . .' He covered his face with his hands and began to sob, while Stanwick watched him with a stolid expression.

'When were you last in touch with your parents?' he asked when Martin had regained control of his emotions.

'I used to speak to my mother on the telephone once or twice a week. The last occasion was on Sunday evening.'

'Did she seem all right then?'

'Yes.'

'No talk of suicide or anything like that?'

'Definitely not.'

'Did you also speak to your father on that occasion?'

'No.'

'Did your mother have any worries that you were aware of?'

'No.'

'Did she and your father get along all right?'

'They had their ups and downs like most married couples. My father was a strong personality and it was my mother who had to make most of the compromises, but she was used to that.' He gave Stanwick an anguished look. 'None of what I'm saying will get into the newspapers, will it?'

'I assure you the papers won't learn anything from me.' He paused. 'I don't go in for leaks to the press,' he added firmly. Martin became convulsed by further sobbing and Stanwick waited for him to recover his composure before going on. 'Your mother doesn't appear to have left a note, Mr Cuckfield. It's possible, of course, that she and your father had a quarrel and she took her life immediately afterwards. It's also possible that she did leave a note, which your father found and removed. We shan't know until he re-appears.' He paused. 'Do you think he may have killed himself?'

'I can't believe he would . . . but how can one ever know who might take his own life?'

Stanwick nodded. 'I'm aware that the most seemingly unlikely people are capable of committing suicide. If your father were to kill himself, how do you think he would do it? I know it's a disagreeable question, but I'd be glad of your answer.'

'I would think he'd shoot himself,' Martin said in little more than a whisper.

'With one of his shotguns?' Martin nodded. 'And it would be reasonable to suppose he'd do so either in the house or its vicinity?'

'I . . . yes, I'd think so.'

'I mean,' Stanwick went on, 'he'd be unlikely to put his gun in the car and go driving off into the blue?'

Martin gave a helpless shrug.

'The presumption, therefore, is that he's still alive. But where?'

'I've no idea,' Martin said dully.

'Do you happen to know the registration number of his car?'

'Why?'

'Why what, sir?' Stanwick said with a frown.

'Why are you so keen to trace him?' Martin asked with sudden fierceness. 'Disappearing isn't a crime, as far as I know. Isn't my poor mother's death sufficient without your trying to make a mystery out of it?'

Stanwick looked pained. 'I'm sorry you feel that way, Mr Cuckfield. I assure you I'm doing no more than my duty— '

'What the hell is a detective chief inspector doing on what's a clear case of suicide?'

'I'm also investigating two murders, concerning which I've interviewed your parents. I think that answers your question.'

'They've nothing to do with my mother's death.'

'Haven't they? You may be right, but I still need to find your father. Surely you see, Mr Cuckfield, that recent events could have a bearing on what's happened here today?'

'I suppose so,' Martin said in a grudging tone, 'but I totally reject the assumption that my father's disappearance is related to any crime.'

'I'd have expected you to be as anxious as anyone to have him found. After all, he may be in need of medical attention. It's in his own interest that we find him quickly. I propose to alert hospitals, as well as other police forces. Will you be remaining here for a while?'

171

'Yes. I have a lot of phone calls to make and it'll be easier to do it here. I must let my minister know what's happened.'

He was considerably more composed than he had been when he arrived and Stanwick guessed that facing the compulsion of practical priorities had helped to steady him.

Leaving him to make his telephone calls, Stanwick returned to headquarters to organise the search for Sir Denzil. Events at Greenborough Court had shaken him, too, and he felt like somebody treading a dangerously slippery path.

32

Rosa heard the news via one of Margaret's increasingly regular phone calls. She had just returned to the office after a morning in court when Stephanie announced that Mrs Pickard was on the line.

'It's as if somebody has put a curse on Greenborough,' Margaret said at the conclusion of her recital of events. 'Once the news was out, I need hardly tell you that it went round the village with the speed of light. Ana, one of their Portuguese staff, told Mr Witherspoon who had gone to the house to repair something or other. And telling Mr Witherspoon is the equivalent of broadcasting it on the World Service.'

'Is there any doubt that Lady Cuckfield did commit suicide?'

'You mean, could her husband have killed her? It doesn't sound like it, though I'm sure that won't prevent the spread of rumours to that effect. But what do you think has happened to Sir Denzil?'

'That's like asking a lawyer to prophesy the outcome of a case. It all depends. Until one knows why he's disappeared, the question has as many answers as you care to think of. But it's an extremely interesting development.'

'You think it could help Adrian?'

'It's too early to tell. Once more, it all depends.'

'I feel sad about Lady Cuckfield's death. I wonder what drove her to take her life.'

Rosa believed she held a clue, but wasn't yet prepared to give voice to her views. From a practical point of view she was much more intrigued by Sir Denzil's disappearance.

She was due to have dinner with Peter that evening and looked forward to canvassing his opinion of events at Greenborough Court.

While she was waiting for him to call for her in his car, she switched on the radio in the hope of hearing further news. But there was merely a two-sentence report, with the suggestion that Sir Denzil might be suffering from amnesia.

'I've booked at Oscar's Place,' Peter said as Rosa got into the passenger seat beside him. 'I've said we want a quiet table as we have business to discuss.'

It was a French restaurant with *fin de siècle* décor and excellent food. A further virtue in the judgement of many of its clients was an absence of background music. It was situated in Covent Garden and should anyone ever comment on the lack of musical decibels, Oscar was apt to wave an arm at the door and say, 'If you want music, the opera house is along the road. But if you want to eat well, you have come to the right place.'

'I'm confused, Peter,' Rosa said, as she sipped a Campari and orange juice. 'I can understand Lady Cuckfield committing suicide, but I'd never have expected him to run away.'

'He may have felt conscience-stricken about her death.'

'Huh! From all accounts he treated her like chattel. He's an egotistical tyrant. And a murderer.'

'Where do you think he's gone?'

'He's obviously hiding somewhere.'

'Or he may have done a Lord Lucan. Managed to do away with himself without leaving a trace. You could be wrong about Sir Denzil,' Peter went on as he set about a bowl of *moules marinières*.

'In what way?'

'That he's not a murderer, but an innocent and unloved man caught in a web of suspicious circumstances.'

'I'm sure I'm not wrong,' she said with quiet conviction. 'He had both opportunity and motive.'

'What motive?'

'I think he was being threatened with blackmail over something in his past.'

'Have you found out what?'

'Let's say I have more than the mere glimmer of an idea.'

'Is that all you're going to tell me?'

'Yes.'

'OK, little Rosa, I won't press you. But promise me you'll take care.'

She put out a hand and took hold of one of his.

'I promise,' she said, giving him a grateful look.

33

Mr Seale of the CPS fixed Stanwick with one of his mournful stares.

'I've had a very disturbing report from the laboratory,' he said in a tone which matched his expression. 'That's why I asked you to come over immediately. The lab's handwriting expert is of the opinion that the final entry in Atherly's notebook was not made by the same hand as made the other entries. He had the statement written by Atherly in respect of finding Wells' body for comparison purposes and is quite definite in his view.' Stanwick remained grimly silent and Seale went on, 'Atherly didn't have a very educated hand and at a superficial glance, the final entry bears a resemblance to other writing in the book, but it doesn't stand up to scientific examination.' He sighed. 'So, it looks very much as if somebody has tampered with the notebook. To say that this casts doubt on the case against Pickard is an understatement. It deals it a fatal blow. Miss Epton has already asked to see the notebook and we're bound to let her have the handwriting report. I realise this puts you in an embarrassing position, Chief Inspector, and that you'll want to make your own enquiries into the matter, but I wouldn't wish you to think there can be any sort of cover-up. Indeed, I'm sure you're of the same mind.'

While Seale had been speaking, Stanwick's expression had remained unchanged. It was like a hovering thundercloud.

He knew that Sergeant Travis belonged to a school who thought it all right to gild the lily where the evidence was thin. Unhappily, it was a single short step between that and actual fabrication of evidence. Nobody apart from Travis had had the opportunity to tamper with the notebook. He had gone to see Mrs Atherly and had returned triumphant with it.

Beneath his breath and without any change of expression, Stanwick heaped curses on his sergeant's head in the most colourful language at his command. If suspicion became fact, Travis had not only destroyed his career, but had let down the force to which he belonged and handed the public a further stick with which to belabour the police in general.

'Leave everything with me, sir,' Stanwick said, getting to his feet. 'You don't need to inform Miss Epton immediately, do you?'

'Depends on how you construe immediately,' Seale said with a smile that withered and died under Stanwick's gaze.

As he drove away from the CPS office, Stanwick wondered what he had done to displease the normally benign deity who watched over him. It was not that his life was a permanent bed of roses, but he wasn't used to such a succession of disturbingly unforeseen events.

He had one quick enquiry to make on his way back to headquarters. Parking outside Mrs Atherly's cottage, he walked up to the front door and rapped on it.

'Who is it?' a voice called out.

'Detective Chief Inspector Stanwick, Mrs Atherly. May I come in?'

'The door's not locked,' she answered.

'Sorry to come back again,' he said as he entered the kitchen where she was sitting as usual. 'But something's happened and I'm hoping you can help me.'

'You certainly look worried,' she said, peering at him.

'Do you remember Detective Sergeant Travis coming to see you and taking possession of a red notebook Joe used?'

'Of course I remember.'

'Where was it?'

'In his jacket pocket where I said it was, but your sergeant couldn't find it and I had to go upstairs myself. I told him he hadn't looked properly.'

'How long was he looking for it before saying he couldn't find it?'

'A good five minutes. I couldn't think what he was up to.'

Unfortunately, Stanwick could.

He arrived back at headquarters feeling even more sick at heart.

'Is Sergeant Travis in?' he asked, on his way up to his office.

'Left about forty minutes ago, sir. Said he was going to Gatwick.'

'What, the airport?' Stanwick asked in a startled voice.

'I imagine so, sir. Not much else there.'

He reached his office to find a scrawled note on his desk. It read: 'Sir D.C.'s car found at Gatwick. Am on my way. Will call from there.'

It was an hour later that the call came through.

'Travis here. Did you find my note?'

'Yes.'

'Well, it's Sir Denzil's car all right. It was parked on the top floor of one of the short-term carparks. Locked and no sign of blood-stains. It's pretty obvious he left it and caught a plane. Where to is anyone's guess. I'm making enquiries at various airline desks, but without much hope. It's far too easy these days for people to slip in and out of countries without authorities being any the wiser.'

'Who discovered the car?' Stanwick asked.

'A security officer doing his rounds. He'd noticed it two days ago and was surprised to see it still there. It costs the earth to leave a car in the short-term parks for any length of time. Anyway, he noted the number and later discovered it had been circulated. After that, things moved fairly quickly. I got the message after you'd left to go and see the CPS. Incidentally, what did he want this time? He hasn't got another attack of cold feet, has he?'

'I'll tell you when you get back.'

'I sometimes wonder whose side he's on. Life was better before the Crown Prosecution Service was created. Not perfect, but definitely better.'

'Come and see me as soon as you get back,' Stanwick said curtly and rang off.

The discovery of Sir Denzil's car had done nothing to lift his spirits. The post mortem examination of Lady Cuckfield had confirmed that she had died of barbiturate poisoning, as a result of taking a massive overdose of sleeping tablets, and though he would need to question Sir Denzil about her death, it now seemed a less pressing matter than the conduct of his sergeant who had almost certainly forged a piece of evidence.

He was especially upset as he felt he should have had his own suspicions aroused by the fortuitous discovery of the notebook. He knew Travis was not above a bit of knavery and he castigated himself for not having been more vigilant. Admittedly, he had been under considerable pressure at the time, but that didn't excuse him. As the officer in charge of the investigation, he must be ready to answer awkward questions.

It was the day after delivering the notebook to the CPS that Seale had expressed his own doubts and Stanwick had agreed it should be sent to the laboratory for examination. He had also agreed that no officer, apart from himself, should be aware of what was being done. By then he had realised that there was only one person who could have been involved.

He had decided that the fairest course was to confront Sergeant Travis with the situation before bringing it to the notice of his own superiors. After that, it would be up to them what to do.

The murder charge against Pickard would almost certainly be dropped. As to the other charge, he hoped it would be quietly buried.

Wherever he looked, he could see only trouble.

34

That same day Rosa was about to leave the office and go home when Ben, who was the self-appointed bearer of tidings, waylaid her.

Waving an evening paper, he said, 'I see old Sir Denzil Cuckfield's car has been found, Miss E. In one of the carparks at Gatwick. That tells a story, doesn't it?'

'You mean that he's flown the country? It could be a bit of bluff. You shouldn't jump to conclusions, Ben.'

He grinned. 'Bet you he's skipped.'

'Does it say anything else?'

He shook his head. 'Just that they've found his car and are still looking for him.'

'Well, thanks for letting me know, Ben. It's interesting news.'

It was, indeed, Rosa reflected, as she drove home. If you wanted people to believe you had fled the country, an airport was the obvious place to abandon your car. Gatwick was no more than a forty-minute drive from Greenborough, so presented a natural escape route. But somehow Rosa didn't see Sir Denzil taking flight in that way.

She had been home about two hours, had cooked herself supper and was settling down to read her papers for court the next day, when her telephone rang.

'Is that Miss Rosa Epton?' a male voice enquired when she lifted the receiver. Her caller sounded nervous.

'Rosa Epton speaking,' she said.

'This is Martin Cuckfield, Miss Epton. I believe you're defending Pickard on a murder charge?'

'That's correct.'

'The point is, he didn't do it. I wanted you to know that.'

'Do you mean you have evidence that would secure his acquittal?' Rosa asked eagerly.

'You could put it that way.'

'When can I meet you, Mr Cuckfield? The sooner the better from my point of view. Are you in London?'

'No, I'm staying down at Greenborough Court for a few days. Our London flat has become impossible, with reporters camped outside every day. My wife has taken the children away to friends in the country and I'm . . . I'm trying to cope with the aftermath of recent events. It's been a terrible time.'

'I'm sure it has. I was very sorry to hear of your mother's death.'

'I don't believe I'll ever get over it. I was devoted to her. As for my father, I fear he may have had a brainstorm. I hope he's found for all our sakes. It's not much fun staying here with all the reminders of my parents around me. But there are so many things to be attended to I felt I should be on the spot. And the press are less intrusive here.'

'So when can I see you?' Rosa asked, trying to keep a note of impatience out of her voice.

'I'm not sure when I'll be back in town. It all depends on what happens in the next few days.'

'I could drive down to Greenborough any time. What about tomorrow evening?'

'It isn't that urgent, is it?'

Rosa could sense him backtracking. But as far as she was concerned, there was total urgency. It was vital to find out what he knew and to translate an ephemeral telephone conversation into something of practical value to her client.

'Give me a call tomorrow and I'll tell you how I'm fixed,' he went on.

'You're quite definite that Adrian Pickard didn't murder Atherly?'

'Yes.'

'And can produce evidence to that effect?'

'Call me tomorrow. I won't let you down. I've told you your client is innocent.' His voice seemed to crack and he disconnected before Rosa could push him further.

Afterwards, Rosa speculated about his call. She even wondered whether his father had been in touch with him since his disappearance. Speculation, however, is seldom fruitful and though she was excited by his declaration that Adrian was innocent, she was deeply frustrated by his refusal to be more explicit.

If necessary, she must be prepared to force the issue. She couldn't just sit back and wait.

Peter called her the next morning as she was about to leave for the office. She wasn't surprised to learn that he had already arrived at his, for she knew he regarded early morning as the best time for phoning his Far Eastern clients.

Rosa told him of Martin Cuckfield's call the previous evening.

'I'll drive you down,' he said immediately.

'It might frighten him off if he sees me arriving with an escort.'

'I'm not suggesting holding your hand when you get there, but I'd like to be around. You certainly can't go alone.'

'I don't yet know I'm going at all. I have to call him and find out.'

'If you don't go, you may discover he's had second thoughts, so the sooner you go, the better.'

Which was near enough her own feeling.

It was a day when she found it almost impossible to concentrate on anything other than her visit to Greenborough Court, though whether any meeting would actually take place seemed to become more doubtful as the day progressed.

Her first attempt to call Martin Cuckfield produced an answer in fractured English that he was out.

'Not here. Out,' the voice went on repeating as she tried to find out when he was expected back.

At lunchtime she tried again only to be met with the same unsatisfactory response. And when she tried twice more in the course of the afternoon there wasn't any answer at all. Just before six o'clock she made another attempt to get through, but without success. When she rang Peter's number to tell him their journey would be a waste of time, his answering machine invited her to leave a message. Shortly afterwards he arrived to pick her up.

He listened to what she had to say before announcing, 'Let's be on our way. The odds are he'll be there. He's obviously teetering on the edge of a nervous breakdown, but finding you on his doorstep will help to concentrate his mind.'

'And if he's not there?'

'We'll return tomorrow. But he will be there.'

'Why are you so sure?'

'My oriental instinct. It's the same as feminine intuition.'

Seventy-five minutes later they turned into the drive of Greenborough Court. A fitful moon, which was playing hide and seek with the clouds, silhouetted the house ahead. There was no light coming from any of the windows.

Peter pulled up short of the house and switched off the car lights.

'We're behaving like a couple of conspirators, rather than innocent visitors,' Rosa observed uneasily.

'Let's go closer. It's the sort of house where they have those great heavy curtains that keep out evil spirits. There may be a chink of light.'

Holding hands, they approached the house and had just reached the porch when a light was suddenly switched on. It cast a yellowish glow through the glass panel above the front door.

'I told you he'd be at home,' Peter observed in a satisfied tone.

'I'll ring the bell,' Rosa said. 'You go back to the car.'

She was feeling more and more ill at ease and wished she had phoned from a call box in the village.

'Hang on a moment, I think there's a light on in that room the other side of the front door. There may be a gap in the curtains. You wait here.'

Peter flitted from her side and Rosa watched him go right up to the window and press his face against the glass. He seemed to possess the eyes of a cat and to be able to move with the same stealth. Half a minute later he returned to her side.

'I'm going to ring the front door bell,' Rosa said firmly. 'If we're discovered lurking out here, someone'll send for the police. If they haven't already done so.'

'Take it easy,' Peter whispered. 'Martin Cuckfield's there all right. He's sitting at a desk, but something's wrong.'

'What do you mean?' Rosa asked in alarm.

'He's sitting staring as if he's seeing a ghost. He looks terrified. Unfortunately I could only see a thin slice of the room.'

'Perhaps there's another window.'

Peter nodded keenly. 'I'll go and look.'

'I'm coming with you.'

As they tiptoed past the one through which Peter had peered, it seemed to Rosa that the scrunch of gravel must be heard. It was like some exaggerated noise on a soundtrack.

Turning the corner of the house they found themselves on a soft grass verge with a flower bed against the wall.

'You're right,' Peter said excitedly. 'There is another window.'

It was narrower than the one in front, but there was a lighted 'V' where the two halves of the curtain met.

'We need a ladder,' Peter said. 'Otherwise we're not going to be able to see in.'

'We are if you lift me up,' Rosa said.

After a second's pause, Peter bent forward and she clambered on to his shoulders. With all the care of a circus performer he slowly straightened up and stepped closer to the window. A few fraught seconds later he moved back and returned Rosa to terra firma.

'Could you see anything?' he whispered.

Rosa nodded. 'It's Sir Denzil in there with him. And Peter, he's got a gun.'

'Are you sure?'

'He's facing Martin across a desk and pointing a gun straight at him.'

35

'It's just possible the front door isn't locked,' Peter said after a pause.

The outer porch door was open but the inner door proved to be firmly secured.

'We'd better find a phone and call the police,' Rosa said in a worried voice.

'Leaving Sir Denzil to shoot his son and disappear before help arrives?'

'What do you suggest then?'

'We need to cause a diversion,' Peter remarked thoughtfully. 'I know, I'll hurl a brick through the window and at the same time you ring the bell and bang on the door.'

It struck Rosa as a risky and far from faultless plan, but she had no alternative to suggest. She could only pray that it wouldn't lead to another death.

Peter, who had left her side, now reappeared holding a large white stone, a number of which were used to delineate the boundary of the driveway.

'This should do the trick,' he said. 'Go and stand in the porch and as soon as you hear the sound of breaking glass, ring the bell, thump on the door and generally raise hell. OK, little Rosa?'

'Yes.'

He bent forward and gave her a quick kiss.

'It's our best way of saving Martin Cuckfield's life. Our only way.'

As Rosa positioned herself at the door, she felt that her heartbeats must be audible in the village and beyond.

One moment the night was silent, apart from an owl talking to itself, the next it reverberated to the sound of splintering glass. Rosa pressed the bell as she had never pressed a bell before and with her other hand banged on the door. A few seconds later, Peter joined her in the assault.

'I haven't heard a shot,' he said. 'I think our plan has worked. With luck, Martin has ducked out of harm's way.'

A door slammed somewhere inside the house and then silence reigned again. But not for long. They heard a chain rattle against the inner frame of the front door, followed by the sound of a key being turned in a lock. The door opened abruptly to reveal Sir Denzil, silhouetted against the hall light, pointing his gun straight at Peter's head.

'What the hell's going on?' he shouted angrily. He peered at the two apprehensive faces confronting him. 'Haven't I seen you before?'

'Where's your son?' Rosa asked, surprised to find her voice actually worked.

'If you don't leave immediately, I'll send for the police.' He waved the gun at them in a menacing fashion.

'Stop blustering,' Rosa said. 'I demand to see your son. I have an appointment with him.'

'I remember now, you're the solicitor representing that fellow Pickard. I saw you at the fête.' He looked suddenly old and tired. 'Why are you here? It's time you did some explaining.'

'You, too,' Rosa said. 'A great deal of explaining.'

'I don't owe you any explanation.'

'I wish to see Martin,' Rosa said again, fearing that their doorstep confrontation was reaching a stalemate.

'Why?'

'Because he called me yesterday evening and said he knew my client was innocent of murder.'

Sir Denzil frowned. 'He said that?'

'Yes.'

'Did he tell you how he knew?'

'No, but I assumed he had evidence as to who had killed Atherly.'

'But he didn't tell you who that person was?'

'No. But I could guess.'

'And what was your guess?' Sir Denzil enquired, swinging the gun round and levelling it at Rosa.

Before she could reply, Peter had moved in front of her.

'That it's you who killed both Harry Wells and Joe Atherly,' he said.

Sir Denzil stared at Peter as he might have at a boy who had just pelted him with a snowball.

He has nothing to lose by committing another murder, Rosa

thought. You can only serve one sentence of life imprisonment. Curiously, she no longer felt frightened, but as if she was having a macabre dream which would be shattered when he pulled the trigger.

Turning abruptly on his heel, Sir Denzil said, 'I think you'd better come in.'

The air of unreality increased as they followed him into the house, glancing warily about them. Sir Denzil led the way into the study. The desk was still solidly there, but there was no sign of Martin. The stone that Peter had hurled through the window lay where it had fallen.

'Where's Martin?' Rosa asked. 'We know he was here.'

'He's obviously gone,' Sir Denzil said in an unfriendly tone. He was still holding the gun, but no longer pointing it at his visitors.

'Is that thing loaded?' Peter said.

'Certainly it is. Want me to show you?'

'I'd much sooner you unloaded it.'

Sir Denzil laughed unpleasantly, but broke the gun and removed two cartridges which he put in his pocket.

Then, laying the weapon on top of the desk, he said, 'So you think I'm a murderer? Most of the village does. But that's because I've never sought cheap popularity. Anyway, what makes you think I killed Wells and Atherly?'

'They were blackmailing you,' Rosa said. 'It's my belief that Atherly took over as blackmailer after you'd murdered Wells.'

'Presumably you think you know the cause of the blackmail,' he said coldly. 'Go on, tell me. The gun's not loaded, so I'm not about to shoot you.'

'It goes back to when you were a pupil at Warren Hall,' Rosa said. 'A boy called Stephen Willett disappeared and a man named Price was charged with his murder, but was acquitted.'

'You're not suggesting, I hope, that I killed Willett?' His tone was grimly sarcastic.

'No.'

'Good. I may have been a precocious child, but not that precocious. Go on.'

'Price had a girl-friend called Norma Kirk, who was pregnant at the time of his trial. She later gave birth to a daughter who was adopted when she was only a few weeks old. I found that out because I followed a hunch and went to St Catherine's House. Price later committed suicide and Norma Kirk, who had left the district before her child was born, married a man named Keith Wells, by whom she had three sons, the youngest being Harry who was murdered here in Greenborough a few weeks ago. His mother who had been in ill health for years died only last week.'

An unnatural silence had fallen in the room, with Sir Denzil as watchful as an animal observing its prey.

Rosa went on, 'I realise I'm telling you what you already know, but I'm doing so to indicate that the case against you is more than mere surmise.'

'I'm still waiting to hear the subject of this supposed blackmail,' he said.

'You were being threatened with exposure,' Rosa replied, meeting his hostile gaze.

'I don't follow you,' he said with a sudden frown.

'Harry Wells had discovered he had a half-sister,' she said. 'Your wife.'

For what seemed an eternity, he stared at her, his expression as blank as a rock face.

'So!' he said, at length. 'So that's it! That's why you believe I was being blackmailed? That's why I committed murder? In order that the world shouldn't find out that my wife was the illegitimate child of a murderer?'

'Except that Price wasn't a murderer. He was acquitted. Moreover, there's living proof that Stephen Willett grew up to father a son of his own.'

'I'm not interested in what happened to Willett,' he said. 'But I'll tell you one thing, young lady, you're not as clever as you think you are.'

Rosa was disconcerted by something in his tone, but was determined not to become side-tracked.

Fixing her with a look in which disdain and anger fought for supremacy, he went on, 'Let me now tell you something else. It's true that my wife was the daughter of Norma Kirk and the man Price, but that's not the dark secret you believe I've been living with all my married life.' He paused for a moment. 'As a matter of fact I only found out after my wife had taken her life. She left a note telling me the truth about her parentage. I knew she had been adopted as a baby by people called Gourlay who lived up in

Derbyshire. The arrangements were made by Mrs Gourlay's sister who lived in Greenborough and knew the Kirks. I met Joyce at a dance and fell in love with her. As far as I was concerned that was all that mattered. Her adoptive parents were devoted to her and she to them. It was a long time after we were married that she learnt who her real mother was, though she never told me. Mrs Wells wasn't even a name to me before I read my wife's note. It was everyone's misfortune that she had a son who discovered the identity of his half-sister and decided to exploit the situation. As for Atherly, he had too long a memory and drew his own conclusions after Wells' death.'

'If what you say is true, why did you run away after Lady Cuckfield's death?'

'I did not run away,' he said with a spurt of anger. 'I've never run away in my life.'

'Call it what you will, it comes to the same thing. You left home, skedaddled, disappeared.'

'Discovering my wife dead was shock enough, but the note she left compounded the shock a thousand times. I sleep soundly and it wasn't till I awoke around six thirty that I discovered Joyce dead. I needed to have some time on my own to think. I left my car at Gatwick to confuse the trail and went to stay with a retired gamekeeper who lives alone on Exmoor and where I knew I wouldn't be troubled by anybody.'

'And this evening you returned,' Rosa said.

'I'd always intended returning. I knew it was the Portuguese couple's half day and I guessed I'd find Martin here. The time had come for him and me to have a talk.'

'Is that why you threatened him with a loaded gun?'

He made a gesture of impatience. 'If you and your Chinese friend hadn't come blundering in, everything would have been settled by now.' In a grim tone he went on, 'The reason my wife took her life was because she felt she was in some way to blame for her son having become a murderer.'

186

36

It took the police some time to identify Martin Cuckfield. His car was a burnt-out wreck and his charred body was still strapped into the driver's seat.

It seemed that the car had failed to take a left-hand bend, had gone out of control and hit the parapet of a railway bridge, after which it had ended up in a ditch and burst into flames.

A subsequent post mortem revealed that the deceased's blood alcohol level was six times over the limit. An empty Vodka bottle beneath the driver's seat told its own story. Evidence was given at the inquest that the dead man had recently been under enormous stress. His mother to whom he had been devoted had taken her own life and this had come on top of a period of exceptional strain in his ministerial career.

In the absence of contrary evidence, the coroner recorded a verdict of accidental death and everyone let out a sigh of relief, not least those who were privy to details which didn't emerge and which, had they done so, would have opened old wounds and caused great distress to a number of innocent people.

The charges against Adrian Pickard were dropped; the burglary on the grounds that the prosecution accepted it couldn't prove a criminal intent and the murder charge because of laboratory evidence which cast doubt on the validity of a vital exhibit.

As for Sergeant Travis, he took early retirement, which was certainly the better of the two alternatives that faced him.

Rosa felt so chastened by her own misreading of the evidence that she was prepared to co-operate in what Peter referred to as Operation Tidying-Up.

She bitterly reproached herself for having been so blind. It had simply not occurred to her that everything that pointed at Sir Denzil also pointed at his son. Moreover, as a government minister, Martin was even more vulnerable to Wells' blackmail. Had it ever become public that his maternal grandfather had stood trial in a notorious murder case, it would have been the effective end of his career. And Rosa could now only guess at whether

187

his phone call was prompted by an over-burdened conscience or was a desperate – and futile – effort to buy more time.

It was a few weeks after Adrian's discharge that Rosa and Peter drove down to Greenborough for Sunday lunch. She was still in a chastened mood.

'We're selling up and leaving,' Margaret said as they sat over drinks while Adrian was in the kitchen putting the finishing touches to their meal.

'Where are you going?' Rosa asked, not really surprised by the decision.

'We're booked on a cruise and shan't make any plans until we get back. It's a long cruise.' She gave Rosa a wry smile. 'I understand Greenborough Court is on the market.'

'Sir Denzil's leaving?' Rosa said.

'Apparently. Can't say I blame him after all he's been through. I doubt whether the village will shed many tears over his departure.'

'Where's he off to?'

'Argentina. He can't get much further away than that. He has a brother-in-law out there.'

A sound of cheerful whistling came from the kitchen.

'Adrian seems to have bounced back completely,' Rosa remarked.

'But of course,' Margaret said. 'He's achieved the purpose which drew him to Greenborough. With your help. It's ironic to think that Sir Denzil and Adrian's father were once boys together at Warren Hall.'

Peter, who had been gazing out of the window, suddenly turned and said, 'How would it be, little Rosa, if you and I ran a village post office?'

Rosa blinked. 'I never know how serious he's being when he says things like that,' she remarked to Margaret.

'Completely serious,' he said.

She went over to the window and gave him a quick kiss on the cheek.

'I'm sure there's a Chinese saying to cover the situation,' she observed. 'Something like, "When girlfriend down-hearted, buy her post office".'

Peter put an arm round her waist and pulled her into his side and Rosa felt suddenly more at ease with herself.

* * *

As they were leaving Peter turned back for a final word with Margaret. Adrian drew Rosa to one side.

'Thanks to you, Rosa, I've been able to establish my identity,' he said softly. 'I only wish I was left with a happier picture of my father at Warren Hall. He was obviously one of those boys not made for boarding-school and hated the place. To make matters worse, he must often have felt abandoned with his parents out in India. I can understand his falling in with Reuben Flanagan and his family who must have appealed to his non-conforming spirit. It's my guess that it was Flanagan who encouraged him to run away from school and who engineered his departure and afterwards harboured him.' He fell silent as he stared ahead deep in thought.

Eventually, he focused his gaze on Rosa and spoke again in a quietly determined voice. 'I've already made up my mind that I'm going to assume my rightful name. I want to be known as Adrian Willett. I owe it to my father.'